EROGENOUS ZONE

CROGENOUS ZONE
A Sexual Voyage

Edited by
Jessica Tilles

Publishing

Published by
Xpress Yourself Publishing, LLC
P. O. Box 1615
Upper Marlboro, Maryland 20773

EROGENOUS ZONE: A SEXUAL VOYAGE. Copyright © 2007 by Xpress Yourself Publishing

All Xpress Yourself Publishing, LLC's titles are available at special quantity discounts for bulk purchases for sales, promotions, premiums, fund-raising, educational or institutional use.

Special book excerpts or customized printings can also be created to fit specific needs. For details, write to Xpress Yourself Publishing, LLC, P.O. Box 1615, Upper Marlboro, MD 20773, Attn.: Special Sales Department.

ISBN-10: 0-9792500-4-8
ISBN-13: 978-0-9792500-4-0

Printed in the United States of America

Cover and Interior Designed by
The Writer's Assistant
www.thewritersassistant.com

Xpress Yourself Publishing World Wide Web site address is
www.xpressyourselfpublishing.org

CONTENTS

CONTENTS (CON'TD)

INTRODUCTION

Erogenous Zone

Erogenous Zones are those areas of the body that arouse sexual desire. Erogenous has two general meanings: 1) The genitals or breasts, which when stimulated produce pleasurable sensations, and 2) Those areas of the female body which men find sexually arousing and which women alter or adorn to attract the male eye.

Erogenous Zone: A Sexual Voyage will prove to be an erotic anthology as richly diverse as it is startlingly original, with delicacy and daring, rapacity and repose, exultant lyricism and icy lucidity—from the warmly sensual to the explosively cutting-edge, from the playfully amoral to the profoundly moving, this sensual collection will tease, touch, seduce, arouse, inspire you, and get you hot!

Within the pages of this sexual voyage, lies some of the hottest, sensual stimulating stories you will have the pleasure of reading—a collection of beautifully written pieces, that will surely make you hot by tickling your erogenous zone and through mental stimulation.

So, quickly pour your favorite libation, kick off your shoes and cuddle up with your partner. You, my friend, are in for one hot, lovemaking, night!

Jessica Tilles
July 16, 2007
10:11pm

JESSICA TILLES
WILLIAM FREDRICK COOPER

I Want to Fuck You
(No One Has To Know)

HIM: It need scarcely be said that the sex most of us experience in the real world is more routine than the erotic diagrams in our mind. But I had a feeling the woman seated on the bar stool across the way might be a special exception.

The panther within my core wants to leave the prim and proper at home, for she set off all the alarms in my body. My inner beast, hibernated so long in celibacy, wanted the vision that kidnapped my pupils to awaken its senses. My sex drive, rude and abrasive to the normal nice guy by day, told the gentleman not to go home, but to get the hell out of my body for the night. A hungry lust at my center rumbling, I started to feel the stirring of an animalistic arousal. Rocking me while capturing my mind, freakish thoughts of fantasy leave me by way of my heated gaze.

Mmm, I want to fuck you. Coffee-skinned, someone added just the right amount of milk to her complexion. Every inch of this temptress is in perfect proportion. Her eyes, feline shaped and sparkling, told me that she's freaky too, and seduction is her specialty. Oozing Eros, the way she sipped from her Cosmopolitan with those pouting red, kissable lips sent a telegram to my hard-on. It's message? Let me move and soothe you. Teasing me while revealing a racy secret, _she loves to suck chocolate cumsicles_, they whispered.

1

Damn, I gotta fuck you. The musculature of her deliciously defined legs let me know that if teased and pleased proper, this siren could go all night. Envisioning myself licking the back of her chiseled calves, my lips traced her ankles and knees, searching for a pleasure zone, seeking to bring quiet shouts of sextasy from her. Planting kisses along her inner thighs, the fluent flutter-flicks of my creature from oral space would make her legs buckle as her pussy vibrated.

The pink walls of her honey: Are they just the way I hope they would be? Visualizing her grabbing my head while experiencing clit overload from my cunny-licking class, are her orgasms womb-centered around slow strokes rotating inside of her? Up and down, in circles or from behind, does she want to saddle up and ride, clutching and clenching something stiff and strong with motion muscles?

Damn, the blood vessels of my steel squirm at the thought of feeling her honey. Harder than any calculus problem, if a teacher asked me to come to the board to write an answer, I'd politely take the zero to save myself from embarrassment. Wanting to touch, kiss, and fulfill every sexual wish, I wonder if she can hear the roar of my stare.

HER: Leaving me speechless, a rarity, his approach was smooth. Nothing I'd ever experienced, his silent game was totally unfamiliar. My thoughts were completely jumbled, unable to find words to form a complete sentence. Damn, those eyes. His gaze screaming sexual overtures, yet silent in its appeal, if more men used that approach, there'd be a lot of happy women in this world.

One corner of his mouth was pulled into a slight smile as I felt his eyes roaming, becoming familiar with parts of me that hid behind clothing. Sitting at the bar, I slightly positioned myself, exposing the thick lusciousness of my inner thigh. I wonder if he'll figure out how much I love to have this part of me stroked with a wet tongue. Twitching frantically, my pussy is the radar that zeros in on the bulge between his legs that shouted, "I want to fuck you."

Flickering under the hood of my pleasure zone, I wonder if his tongue has the talent to please someone of such a freaky nature, as myself. Does it tickle and tease with its eagerness to please? Or will the munching melody of his mouth have me humping his face? Damn, he has me feelin' kind of right for him at this instant. Yeah, baby, you can have some, 'cause I wanna fuck you, too.

Chills run deep down to the bone, as I imagine the tip of his nose briskly brushing against the swelling between my thick lips. His tongue licking and lapping the exterior walls of my pussy, I hope he can liberate me from the lonely feeling that has me in this club tonight. Will he enjoy the taste of me? My dreams scream "Yes!" I wonder if he can read my thoughts, he has me thinking up and down, him inside of me, making the unnamable sensations take over my mind, body and soul.

Slipping up and fitting within, can he make my ready reservoir shout 'Amen'? Taking my order with that sexual stare, I felt the questions escape him. *How do you like your love? May I take your order? On a platter, anytime and anywhere you want, or does it really matter? Tell me how you like, need and want it.* Leaving those thoughts on the table to ponder as I moved to satisfy my curiosity, I wonder if he penetrates with deep long strokes or rapid pounding. I prefer deep long strokes, slow and steady, so each and every nerve of my honey well can savor the moment. Receiving, and then releasing his steel with my grip, I want to swim in a pool of ecstasy as rippling contractions of sexual bliss engulf me. Yearning to lose control and have disorderly orgasms with him, I want him to probe my slippery oyster until that climatic pearl escapes me, or a multitude of orgasms captures me; whichever comes first. Recovering from his sexual skills, my blissful descent to earth will find him gazing into my eyes, repeating those words, as I feel my love muscles clenching against his dick, "I wanna fuck you."

Noticing me peering at him, the bonfire in his pants grows. I wonder if his girth will expand my opening, or will I not feel it at all. Shit, I don't care, it's been a while, I wanna fuck him too.

HIM: For your lust tonight, I will do most anything. Healing your broken wings if for a brief interval, I want to make the erotic heaven within your earth sing. Needing a key to her lust, I approach the bartender.

"Make sure her glass remains full tonight," I command, enhancing my directive with a crisp Ben Franklin.

"You got it," he complied.

The percussive grooves of Washington, D.C. invade our non-verbal cat-and-mouse game. Those drums and brass knows exactly what I feel. Temporarily removing my eyes from my desire, I scan the dance floor and see women wiggling, backing their thangs up against brothers built like oak-trees, making them cum in their minds. As my thoughts return to that erotic matter at hand, I ask: What is it about leaving the Big Apple for a weekend that removes all inhibitions?

Floating around my core, in fantasy I take my erotic dream girl's hand. Undressing then caressing her, then tasting her center, an enormous sense of urgency overwhelms me. All wishes will become reality later.

But for now, the non-verbal, non-physical two-step will do. Damn, I'm enjoying Martini's, this Maryland club. I hadn't heard the sounds of the early south in a minute. The Go-Go beats have stopped, and the resident deejay, feeling a bit nostalgic, puts on *Hush*, a song from the New Jack Swing Era.

Yup-yup, I think, a la Teddy Riley. Wait, what's this? After rejecting the overtures of many, my temptress has taken to the dance floor with a brother moving like Carlton Banks. What the… Doesn't she still want some of this? Does she still dream of our dance in delight after dark? Doesn't she dream of me tasting her, teasing her, then swirling a magic stick inside of her, fucking her furnace furiously in a frenzied fashion, then slowly stirring strokes within her well of passion?

Oh, now I get it. Silly me, I thought she lost interest. Psyche! Facing me while dancing with him, her movements to music are something to behold. Pressing her long index finger to her lips, she's telling me to hush from afar while she continues working her victim over. Swerving seductively, the swiveling gyrations tell me that I could be hers.

I'm beginning to like this voyeur shit.

Enjoying the limber flexibility of this woman, those chiseled calves pulsate makes me wonder how she likes to ride. Straddling me, would she make my toes curl as I reach for the glorious high of a climax? Squirting torrents within her heaven, does she appreciate milky spurts of satisfaction, or does she prefer a man whose orgasm oozes, so she could milk his masculinity until he cried for his Mama?

Yeah, I betta go get that.

That is, after I enjoy the show.

HER: Is he jealous, watching me dancing with this 70's throwback brother? As I sashay my hips from side to side, I see him watching me. His eyes tell me he wants to fuck me bad. *Damn, Boo, I wanna fuck you too*, I think to myself as I seductively raise my arms in the air, pouting my lips toward him, my eyes focused on the enormous urgency between his legs. Damn, I wanna suck him off. Envisioning me searching that G-spot on his tool with my lips, would it taste like a Tootsie Pop? How many licks of the rich, thick chocolate stick would it take to make him cum?

Kissing him all over and straddling him in my mind, I see us enjoying dinner for two. Knowing sixty-nine is my favorite number—hell, it was the year I was born—I wonder if he would like that too, my thick thighs stretched open as his face is buried in my bush, his tongue flickering against my bead.

Musical melodies from the speakers, loud and vibrating through my core, have me dancing with my desire to fuck him. I would get this brother good too. Bending down toward the floor, wrapping my hands around my ankles, and stroking up my legs, stopping halfway…I looked at him with a wicked smile. Shit, I'd be a naughty girl for him all night long, fucking him so well for so long until his eyes became cyclopean. Knowing my movements are arousing him, he's looking at me, lusting like a wolf in sheep's clothing. Fucking me with those piercing eyes, I wonder if the reality would be hard or slow. Would he start off by licking the bottoms of my feet, working his way up my ankles toward my calve muscles, eventually connecting with the cream that would flow from my pussy down to my thigh and slow-drip onto his long, flickering tongue? My cave is tight. Would he drive into me the way I liked to be penetrated, with deep long strokes, causing my body to heave with pleasure? Would our bodies meet, thrusting up, delightfully dancing to the rhythmic pussy-dick melody that would meld our bodies to one? Or would this tempo change from rhythmic to intense as he neared his release?

Pulling myself up, I raise my skirt high above my perfectly firm thighs, my legs parting, giving him a glimpse of sweetness.

Facing my dance partner, who is getting kicks off of watching me tease another man with my well-orchestrated choreography, I lean forward, and gently shake my tight, naked ass. Looking over my shoulder at him, I want to make sure he is taking in what he will be fucking tonight.

That is, if he makes the first move.

Damn, this erotic game of cat and mouse has me so horny. I am ready for him to take me, but I know the chess game will continue for a tick. Look at him, grinning like the cat that was about to eat the canary. For real, I'm ready to replace that smile with the pleasurable grimace of passion a man gives a woman when the pussy feels too good. And I know mine will. Goodness, I want to look in his eyes while riding him and ask him is he enjoying the muscles clenched around his rod. Squeezing, then, skillfully applying pressure on his steel with my pelvic muscles, I bet he'd like that, a gorgeous woman milking the shit out of the dick. He looks like he would.

Where's his mind at now?

HIM: *Let's stop wasting time.* The lyrics adding to the intrigue, we could have so much fun together. Being hers for this moment in time and her mine, I see us cumming together as an avalanche of arousal bowls us over. The colors of red, violet and blue clouding her vision, every single stroke from my core would make her reach ecstasy. Once we get going, the currents of sexual lust will flow along the shores of physical gratification. Seeing her moan and starting to feel it in my mind, her orgasms would be violent, yet beautiful.

Yeah, I need to run up in that. Temperature rising in my heart to a boiling point, It's time to step up to the plate and make this happen.

Walking across the dance floor, I feel her eyes watching my every stride. Connecting glances, I nod in appreciation of her clothed striptease.

My baby can move that ass.

7

Let's see what she can do with a pro now.

Whispering in the disc jockey's ear while greasing his palm with a twenty, the pied piper of foreplay has another player in the game. Smiling, he fulfills my request.

Hush is replayed.

There won't be any hushing now.

Approaching her, the lyrics speak for me. Even Carlton Banks, the rhythmless wonder that needs to dance to Tom Jones' songs, steps away from the heat. Seeing the obvious chemistry between us, he simply returns to Bel-Air, his barstool, as I take her hand.

"Baby, you're mine tonight," I whisper as the groove fills the nightclub once more. No, I'm not one of these brothers feeling like they own all the pussy in a room. But there are some instances where two animals, uniquely connected, know that their bodies will come together for a passionate mating. In short, there are just some people in the world that you just have to fuck. Try as you might to avoid the surging inevitability, the hunger reeking from the pores of hungry souls wears the resistance thin. You and this person must connect sweat and shoulders, lips and limbs, musk, muscles and magical moans of passion. Feeling compelled to move with her gentleness, then, shoot hot spurts of white lava within her sugar walls, it is your obligation as a man to bring many screams of delight from her. This woman was one you just had to have.

"I know," she replied seductively.

Apparently, she agrees.

Fuck getting to know each other through small talk. Fuck even asking for a name at this point. The dance will speak a language our lips won't say: That we'll be good to each other from head to toe. Connecting bodies, she sashays, and backs her ass up to my groin. Wrapping her arms around my neck, I hear the purr of a kitty starving for affection as my tender fingertips and arms become friends with her small waist. The steam between us conquering all degrees of normalcy, I kiss the nape of her neck. Turning to face me, she responds to our syncopated rhythm with a heated gaze.

The silence between us is interrupted with a kiss. Tongues melding magnificently, I stepped into our secret world of desire. Cherry blossoms filling our cocoon, despite the crowd surrounding us, she is my private dancer. The way her lively critter flutters in my mouth is perfect; I want her to do that shit on my nipples later. Connecting with my senses, she knows exactly what to do, and when to do it. A man that she craves is on her menu when the shades go down. The one on one of lust is enticing and enchanting.

Slowing it down, *Is It The Way,* compliments of Jill Scott, comes on. People leave the floor, but there we remain, caught in the web of our wonderful world of two. Swaying seductively to the floor, then back up again, she comes close, the heated stare from her pupils having my body aflame. Adding erotic insult to aroused injury, her fingers graze the hunger at my groin.

"Mmm," she moaned, brushing against the protrusion threatening to burst from its zipper. "You got a lot for me, I see. Can I have some of him later?"

That she asked so sweetly almost made me cum on the dance floor. Blushing, some of the aggression leaves me. But I remained focused.

"Yes, baby. You can."

"I'm not usually this forward, but..."

Stilling her thoughts with a tender peck, "It's okay, baby," I whisper below the sounds of Jill reaching that high score. Is it the way my temptress gushes her desires that makes me glad I'm a man? Or is it the way she moves against me that has my loins

9

aflame with thoughts of her clamping during my climax? Like I said, some people you are destined to sleep with, and try as you might to deny it, it's unavoidable. "I want to fuck you too," I continued.

No, my face didn't feel the sting of an offended palm smack; nor, in the alternative, did the object of my raging hormones leave me on the floor by my lonesome. Fighting her natural impulses, she wants the Siamese song of sexual souls to play as much as I do.

Now, as our lips return to pressing against each other, we savor the soft pucker of the connection of petals. Feeling my nature rise like never before, I notice that she enjoys the feel of my arousal for her, as the original graze against my erection becomes a subtle grope.

"Do you want me to make you cum on the dance floor, sugar, or do you need some place more private?"

Moving against my dick in a slow, circular motion, the answer was obvious to us both as I groaned.

So much for keeping her glass full.

It was time to fill something else up.

HER: The thought of his chocolate tool inside of me, moving every which way, has me hungry as hell. Twitches of anticipation came from my clit as he searched for his card key. I wished he would hurry up, because I wanna fuck him good.

Normally, I'm not the woman who gives up the cookies on the first night. Growing up, guys knew who to call for the quick fix, and never made a play for me, for their sixth sense told them _I wasn't that type of girl_. Little did they know I possessed a risqué, sexual edge to me; an insatiable hunger that could quench the thirst of ten men when ripe. And when I chose to unwrap and unveil the seductress in me to some poor soul, they couldn't

10

hang with the overwhelming hurricane of lust headed their way. I've had them all: Viagra-popping minute men, all-talk, no hip-moving minions, stressed out limp-dick brothas who needed lessons in making love to a woman, or guys that were capable with others but weren't able to tame my voracious appetite. Simply stated, I love being a man's whore behind closed doors.

Tonight's victim will find out.

My thighs, sensuously thick in satisfaction, eagerly awaited him parting and probing me with that tongue I had been waiting for. Wanting to wiggle and woo in excitement, a rush of wetness drenched my crotch. Was this man a chocolate Magellan, an explorer who'll magically map each contour and crevice of my caramel frame? Would he lock his face to my furnace and sensuously suck my sweet spot as if trying to extract some secret information on how the pink kitty is to be petted with his oral flute? Or would my clit become puffy as he made me explode into a billion pieces with deliciously deep thrusting and retreating motions; not to mention the passionate probing from the swollen sword at his groin?

Sucking in a breath while envisioning our bodies soaking wet in sexual sweat, damn I could live for centuries off the tender kisses finding my face. Pecking my forehead, and eyes, then my cheeks and chin, soon he found my brim with his mouth, passionately inserting his tongue as if we were long-lost lovers. Intimately intoxicated by his Drakaar-scented smooth brown skin, I opened his silk black button down, and surrounded his solid frame with my arms as my full lips added to a kissing marathon that seemed like an eternity. Pressing our anxious anatomies together, I felt the heat in his pants rising. Finding a resting place against my navel, it threatened to burst from the cumbersome confines of his zipper. Enjoying the electricity of our embrace while betting against myself, I was confident that once freed, his stiffness would spring out like a jack-in-the-box and touch the moon. Feeling it at my core, a wave of pleasure moved through me.

Somehow, I managed to cut the white-hot sexual tension that threatened to burn the fucking room down.

"Yes Baby," I purred. "I want to fuck you too."

HIM: "You think?" I responded, giggling.

When a sexual connection is as intense as this one is, it's real difficult to have anything else on the mind. It's, hard; real hard. It's as hard as the standing staff at my groin. Unzipping my pants and pulling my dick from its silk boxers, her hands fondled my length, stroking its shaft as if it were a long lost puppy.

Her kiss grew bolder.

"Shit, is this all for me?" she moaned.

"Yes, baby. It's all yours."

I see my fantasy for this evening likes thickness that hooks.

Hearing her cunny speak to my loins once more, I can feel her submission to the sexual story in song about to be composed by a maestro and his magic wand.

Baby, it screamed as our mouths mingled once more, *take me on this voyage to the land of endless, enduring orgasms. I so desperately need, honey. My pussy needs slow strokes at first, to ease the loneliness of missing some delicious dick. Then, as I expand to accommodate your width, Captain Hook, the squishing sounds surrounding your senses is of a pussy wanting you to fuck it well, boo.*

The walls of my vagina are growing wetter by the second, baby. I need you to swivel those loose hips as I rock beneath your hard storm. While you're moving in and out, I'll be up and

12

down, back and forth. Take your time at first; remember, it's been a minute. Then I need you to ignite the fires of complete pleasure within my walls by fucking it so good. Drive that erect commitment deep, then deeper into me with each stroke. Give me all the mileage you own between those gorgeous thighs with each thrust. I'll know when you're getting ready to nut, because the tempo will change from rhythmic to intense. But it better not be too soon. Promise to fuck me good and I'll promise to fuck you good too.

"Message received loud and clear," my dick responded.

Despite the wonderful kiss we were sharing, I craved the unmistakable slurping sounds of my stubborn erection making the heaven between those strong legs sing. My hands, outlining all contours, crevices and intimate intersections of her gorgeous anatomy, began its mission to set her soul on fire. Opening her red blouse, I loved the fact her upturned breasts stood firm. Feeling her ragged breathing, I knew I was on my way to turning her off.

That's right, I said *turning her off.* To properly please a woman, you must turn her on to turn her off. She must turn off the noise of everyday anxieties and daily pressures to relax her mind and enjoy the special moment when bodies craving one another fuse to one. She must turn off all insecurities and forget all experiences, good and bad, so she can be the nastiest woman of your deepest fantasies. She must turn off all fears, so that her pleasure zone can drench your dick upon its entry into her tropical rainforest. Clenching around your length with her squeeze box, contracting and throbbing while moving with you, she must be so turned off to everything around her but you, so that she can feel the force of every single stroke. Like a woman possessed, she must convulse intensely over and over again as orgasms race from her toenails to her temples. All this will happen if you turn her off properly.

Letting my hands satisfy themselves as I pinched those dark, meaty nipples of hers, it was incredibly exciting for her to hear a sigh of anticipation leave her. Decoding my heat correctly, I got a feeling she knows I can hang with her freaky side. With a deliberate slowness, my mouth meandered among her mounds. Attacking her ample cleavage with abandon, my tongue, quickly becoming addicted to this part of her anatomy, fluttered away.

"Oh God, that's it," she breathlessly exalted. Pressing my face against her peaks, I wondered if she really knew I had it all in my sexual shopping mall. Sucking on breasts is akin to an appetizer at Friday's—it only leaves you craving the entrée—the love-juice that comes from her pink pleasure purse. Wanting to tickle, tease, then taste her flaming volcano, I longed to drown from the molten liquid my dining skills would bring.

She'll find that out soon enough. Returning to her pliant petals, our tongues danced together once more. Vibrating with lust as her lips trembled, the face of my fantasy come true wore a twisted mixture of agony and passion as a series of low, lust-laden whimpers and moans left her. Electric sensations radiating through her medium sized-frame, I just knew with those lips she would play the flute at my groin like a virtuoso.

She's gonna get it once I eat her pussy, I thought.

HER: "You look a little hungry, baby," I moaned. "Can I feed you some pussy?"

Shit, where did that request come from? I have never been so aggressive in my life, but all of my inhibitions vanished into the summer air. Hey, I was horny as hell. The talented titillation of that tireless tongue had me craving that creature from the Twilight Zone between my legs. Wanting to rock and willing to ride the rhythm of his oral probing, I allowed him to undress me quickly, then, place me onto the green sofa in

14

his suite. My eyes screwed shut, a dreamy smile appeared as I parted my legs.

Moaning as he rubbed his lean chest over my stomach, the tingling of my cunny indicated impatience. Lord knows, he needed to get down there and suck all the sex from my pink passion-pit.

"Shit, baby," I panted hotly as he explored the lower region of me. Alternatively licking and pecking my inner thighs, he slowly teased the peripheries of my hot points, working all around the spot I so desperately wanted him to munch on. A mere breath of hot air on my fat clit had the feelings of an orgasm flash through me. Boomeranging through my body, bouncing between the tip of my head and the soles of my feet, the exquisite sensation set my body on fire, then, returned to its origin, the labial lips of my vagina, where it rested…temporarily.

Outlining all of pleasure spots, he seemed hungry, determined to lick and suck me dry as he followed my intersections of bliss into a deeper chasm. Wanting to caress his hooked joystick with my pussy muscles, that tireless oral instrument would have to do for now. Hell, it was thick enough.

Groaning as I took hold of it with my grip, the amazement from his surprised pupils aroused me even further. Rotating my hips while flexing, then retreating, the juices within my watery walls started to simmer. Hearing him moan while lapping told me he liked the taste of my kitty.

"Get that shit, motherfucker," I screamed as the tension at my clit grew. Raising my hips off the couch, my back arched beautifully as I rocked. Burying his face in my core, I wanted his tongue, lips and face to meld with the pinkness of my special cleft, bringing from me a lifetime of quiver and quakes. Flicking that fantastic tongue, then vigorously attacking my core with that magnificent mouth, he added more to the pleasure by strumming

15

my love-bud with his nose. Breathless, my head spun with this brother's pussy-eating techniques. His face becoming chums with my hips, my pussy was overflowing with juice. That mind-blowing eruption of shivers, shakes, tremors and trembles began another heavenly ascension as another wave of climax tickled my spine.

Damn, I wanted to flood this man's mouth with all the juice I could muster.

"That's it, baby," I panted as my breaths grew shorter and shorter. Ever so close to that orgasmic haven, I wrapped my legs around this man's head tightly. Goodness, my pussy wanted to sing the praises of this man so bad. Before penetration, my body had never been taken so powerfully.

The orgasms that screamed internally began... to... surface.

The breaths... feel like... I'm losing... Can't control... Yes, baby.... Make mommy cum... shit baby... Yes... Yes... I'm cumming so good for you, baby...oh...oh...

HIM: Feeling those wonderful *ahs* leave her by way of tremors, I knew I had her. Damn, the honey fall from that tasty snatch had an ecstatic effect on me as I drank deeply from her fountain of lust.

Her quiver finally subsided, and the perfect storm left her body, leaving her in a happy state of contentment.

"My goodness," she announced, struggling to release the remnants of her orgasm. Whenever a man curls a woman's body in a fetal position with cunnilingus, all he needs is to penetrate her, and almost instantly, her eyes will become glassy and slit-like. I like that visual, because it lets me know that I'm doing my job.

Her gratification always comes first, as her orgasms are mine as well.

But I must transfer that power for a tick, because I need my rampaging tool polished.

Stroking my shaft, then lowering her face to my groin, the super-horny siren continued her seduction.

Smiling mischievously, "All those orgasms made my mouth dry, boo," my fantasy cum true purred. "Can you help me with that problem?"

Speechless, the seven hooked inches of my erect chocolate screamed what my mouth couldn't say.

Hell, yeah.

Squeezing it tightly while running her free hand along my balls, I moaned as the head of me swelled larger than ever.

My lollipop, her sex drive screamed to my soul, *I can hold onto you this way forever.*

Caressing the shaft of my telescope with those full lips on her pretty face, she ran her mouth along the underside, every now and then deliberately flicking her tongue against my swollen bulb. Teasing me, electric sensations strong enough to illuminate D.C. ran through my body as she massaged the pre-cum that escaped me up and down my dick.

This woman had me begging her to slurp my dark purple tip.

Introducing her mouth to my member, she plunged her head downward, gradually working her lips along the shaft until her mouth felt full. Making loud slurping sounds between famished groans, her lips alternately ran tight and loose around my popsicle. Soon, the movement of my midsection met the motion of her mouth.

Hearing her continued lustful sounds her orifice continued to make, I knew she enjoyed the taming of the tool as much as I did. Instinctively, she knew I needed the release of the sex-repressed knot within me. Wet from the mouth of my sexual

17

seductress, the throbs pulsating through my hardness caused an eruption to brew in the pit of me. Swirling and sucking, she sped up the tempo, slowed that shit so, so down, then, sped up the suction again.

My toes curled. My thighs tightened.

"You do that so good," I moaned.

Pumping into her mouth piston-like now, her throat was bottomless. Damn, this woman could deep-throat a brotha. She was so calm she began rolling her palm against my tightening sacs while gulping, pausing once to peer upward just to make sure she was doing her duty well.

My lover is such a greedy wench, and I love that shit too.

The collision of lust and hunger made the eruption within rise higher. Not being able to help the inevitable feeling if I wanted to, I wouldn't quell the growing sensation of this orgasm even if I could.

Her oral artistry was amazing, and my pulsing probe was about to let her know.

"That's right, baby. Give it to me," she directed between frantic head dives.

My breath got short.

My mouth was dry from all my panting.

My head became dizzy, lightheaded in its sexual contentment.

Ah, shit baby... I gotta untie this knot.

Spurts of warm milk left me as my own storm was in full swing. That my lover reared her head back to capture all of my eruption, made the chocolate rage stream more than ever before. Joining my appreciative cries with groans of her own, she quenched her thirst and, after a seductive wink, recaptured my steel with her mouth.

That alone made more juice escape me; more that she enjoys.

"That's right, baby. Give mama all that shit," she demanded with a sly smile.

Naturally, as one asks, she does receive.

Focusing on my tip, she sucked it dry, causing me to shudder.

"Oh...oh, baby."

HER: "What's the matter, baby you can't take it?" I teased through his pleasurable convulsions while regrouping myself. Feeling his warm seed meet the depths my throat set off another orgasmic explosion. My only regret is that we weren't in the sixty-nine position, for he would have been drenched by more of his hold over my body.

The air of the room, already blanketed with the aroma of sex, needed the mutual scent of his chocolate redwood planted in the core of my tropical jungle. My pussy, hot, hungry, and still tingling from the waves of excitement running through it, required something deep within its walls to keep me from losing all sanity. Wanting to feel the up and down, round and round of his bump and grind, I knew that every contraction of his dick would send waves of pleasure across the synapses of my nerves.

"I want to fuck you now, baby," my chocolate lover announced while pressing both of his thumbs against my clit. "I want to fuck you the way you want to be fucked."

"I need that shit, honey," I announced, already envisioning my hips meeting his halfway as he grunted and groaned.

Pulling him into a passionate kiss, I anxiously sucked his tongue as he removed his thumbs from my pleasure chest.

"I need to feel you now. Please put in," I commanded.

Panting, he quickly rose from the green sofa and covered his steel with latex in record time. Returning to me, I spread my legs in anticipation of what I knew would be powerful strokes. Slowly and gently, my lover rubbed himself against my outer lips, driving me fucking crazy.

My body, shaking already, couldn't wait for entry. The sensation of his dick stirring within my pot of water made my senses boil as he continued teasing me.

"Baby, please fuck me now!"

Slowly, he pushed the head, then the shaft inside of me. Gasping as his hook stretched the contours and crevices of my honey pot, his tempered thrusts were enough to send chills up and down my spine as I lifted my legs high in the air to accommodate him. Varying the pace of his action, he balled me nice and slow first, his circular motion and deep steady strokes finding places I never knew existed in me.

"Yes, baby. Fuck me good with that hooked dick. C'mon, baby," I groaned as I pulled him close. I needed to kiss him in that instance.

Feeling him fully implanted within, I sighed with pleasure.

HIM: "Do you want it open or closed?" she asked through ragged breaths.

I'm glad we dimmed the lights, because my eyes widened in amazement with her question.

Grabbing my ass, she drew me deep, and then deeper as she contracted, then released my steel. Open meant her lust-tube was wide for me. And whenever she did that, I cranked up the tempo of my purpose.

Feeling her fingertips, then long nails raking my back ever so gently, her seductive moans were as rapid as the rhythm inside of her. Moving like a machine in the depths of her heaven, she closed sesame, and instantly, the walls of her honeywell were as tight as a vise. Loving her kegel-control, only an enormous exercise of restraint prevented me from going over the edge. Screwing me back from below, her tightness tugged and pulled at the foundations of my soul as her marvelous midsection met and matched my movements.

Soon, the squishing sounds of a fully aroused pussy had the pulsating pillar of pleasure at my groin throbbing intensely. Thrusting in and out of her gripping walls, the pace of my sexual madness grew frantic.

HER: Fuck, this was some good dick moving inside of me. Looking deep into his eyes, a look of extreme pleasure captured his face as I stuck my hands through my legs past his thrusting tool and lightly squeezed his tightening balls.

"Damn, baby," he moaned, unleashing an animalistic moan while speeding up his stroke.

"Yes, baby," I responded "Fuck me good, baby."

The passion raging like an out-of-control forest fire, our mutual joining grew in rhythm as well. Moving like cartoon characters, the pace turned to feverish pounding on his end, as he impaled me oh so good while sucking on my gumdrop nipples.

I loved that shit, and I let him know that I enjoyed his incredible stamina.

"That's right, Fuck it. Fuck your pussy like you'll never get this again," I screamed in a hoarse voice that was filled with ecstasy. My eyes had tears of pleasure in them.

Feeling an incredible sensation brewing in my stomach, I knew the quivers and quakes of a really fantastic feeling wouldn't stay at my stomach. Spreading through me, my eyes rolled to the top of my head as that hooked organ between his hard thighs and those fucking amazing hips continued its composition. Rocking beneath him, I gave a breathless moan and allowed the incredibly intense orgasm to kidnap my body.

"Shit, baby…You're making me cum so hard….Yes, baby, yes…," I moaned as the long, wild moment of extreme pleasure had me shaking so hard. As another wave of bliss set my body ablaze, I let out an ear-piercing yell so loud I'm sure the whole floor of the hotel must've heard. I didn't care, because Captain Hook delivered a dick-down, a humping that I'd remember for the rest of my days.

Now, Daddy had to cum for Mama real good.

HIM: Savoring the delicious feel of her pussy, while she was screaming, I slowed my roll, dancing within her watery walls as if Rick and Teena were singing _Fire and Desire_ to us. Hugging and kissing her, our tongues matched the synchronicity of our souls.

Feeling her cunny cun-cun tighten around me, I began to rock and buck like a bronco, then, felt my body stiffening once more. The tell-tale rumbling in my dick now brought to the surface, the pressure of another climax moved from the countless muscles of my body through my shaft, threatening to make me blind from the pleasure.

"That's right, baby. Come for Mommy."

Shit, that seductive, nurturing tone sent me over the edge. Closing my eyes, I surrendered to the spasm that made my juices rush from me like an express train. Exploding from the tip of my steel, ribbon after ribbon of my seed flooded my condom as a gigantic convulsion took hold of me. My lover only intensified the pleasure-pain feeling by squeezing hard.

Breathless, we collapsed in total contentment.

Bravely, I spoke. "Jessica, that was fun."

My lover smiled through the darkness. "I know, William, wasn't it?"

"Next year, we gotta do our annual lovers getaway in Bermuda."

"Don't forget the jar of honey," she cooed, "and handcuffs next time. But I must admit, that 'total stranger' fantasy was awesome."

"I had to think of something quick. Get some rest, Jessica. I want some more of you, boo."

"Yes, Baby. I want to fuck you some more, too."

JESSICA TILLES is an award-winning, critically-aclaimed author, publisher, founder, and CEO of Xpress Yourself Publishing, LLC, Poetic Press (an Xpress Yourself Publishing imprint) and The Writer's Assistant. A native of Washington, DC, she is a creative writer in all genres of fiction, with several titles in print: *Anything Goes, In My Sisters' Corner, Apple Tree, Sweet Revenge, Fatal Desire, Unfinished Business* and *Erogenous Zone: A Sexyal Voyage* (an anthology). Jessica is the recipient of the 2003 Memphis Black Writer's Conference's Rising Star Award for Literature and The Jackson Mississippi Readers Club's Contribution to African American Literature Award.

WILLIAM FREDRICK COOPER is the author of the critically-acclaimed novel *Six Days In January,* as well as the award-winning *There's Always A Reason*, a message-delivering, emotional masterpiece many consider the "2007 Book Of The Year" within the African-American Community. An ordinary guy trying to touch lives, hearts and, when writing erotica, bodies, he has contributed to many steamy anthologies and novels such as Zane's *Dear G-Spot: Straight Talk About Sex and Love*, Zane's *Caramel Flava, Sistergirls.com*, and *Twilight Moods: African-American Erotica*. He can reached at his e-mail address: areason006@yahoo.com.

Butterflies

K iana ran her big toe across the grooves of the hot water faucet while she leaned her head back against the bathtub. The steam from the nearly scalding hot water ascended into the air as beads of water danced across her curvaceous leg. Inhaling the scent of the peach-scented candles and the red and white rose petals floating in the tub, she hummed softly to the melody of Musiq's *b.u.d.d.y.* playing on the radio perched on top of the sink. This was the perfect remedy she needed after her last grueling day of sifting through W-2s, 1099-INT forms, and cluttered receipts. Shaking her head in disbelief, Kiana could hardly believe this would be her final tax season with Parker, Hunter and Brennan, LLP, since she was resigning from her job in two weeks.

The bathroom door opened slowly as her husband Gerald entered the room carrying two glasses of champagne and a fruit salad bowl of sliced mangos, pineapples and strawberries on a wooden tray. "Can't get enough of that new Musiq song, huh?" he asked, closing the door with his right shoulder.

She titled her head and smiled. "Mm hmmm," she replied. "You know this is my jam."

Gerald nodded and sat the tray down on the stand.

"Thank you so much, baby," Kiana said, thinking about how sweet it was of her husband to surprise her with a romantic evening that catered to her every desires when she arrived home—from the lovely bouquet of red and white roses symbolizing his love to the candlelit dinner for two featuring some of her favorite dishes. It was romantic and thoughtful gestures that Gerald did for Kiana that made her appreciate and love her husband for the past three years of their marriage.

He removed and hung his robe on the door. "You are so welcome," he replied. His chocolate brown body was chiseled symmetrically from the pecs on his torso all the way down to his massive quadriceps and bulging calves on those long legs.

Kiana sat up and leaned forward. *Fuck the champagne and the fruit salad,* she thought, *I'll take a slice of those tender legs any day.*

He stuck his right foot in the tub. "Dayum, baby! Did you have to make the water so hot?"

"You know that's the way I like it, so quit complaining. Man up!"

Shaking his head, Gerald picked up the glasses and handed them to his wife. He slowly eased his way into the tub behind her while his body adjusted to the hot temperature. "Here's to you, baby," he toasted. "Congratulations on finishing your final tax season!"

"Yeah," Kiana chuckled, sipping her champagne.

"What's up?" Gerald asked, placing his glass outside the tub.

Sitting her glass outside the tub, she reclined her body against his chest. "Just thinking."

"About?"

"The future."

"What about it?"

"I don't know if I should have quit. I mean, it's not easy to change careers nowadays, especially in this economy. With all

25

this talk about the bubble about to burst in the real estate market, maybe it isn't a good time to–"

"Hey," Gerald interjected. "That's fear talking. You gotta cut that shit out."

Kiana tilted her head. "Easy for you to say. Do you know how many hours I'm going to have to put in to be successful? Hell, I know it'll be at least six months before I'll even begin to see an actual paycheck."

"Well, you shouldn't have quit then."

She reached back and smacked him upside his head.

"Ouch!" he yelled.

Kiana laughed. "That's not funny. I'm being serious."

"And so am I," Gerald replied, wrapping his arms around her waist. "Honey, you've got to step out on faith. Ask yourself this question. Did you really want to spend another minute at that accounting firm?"

"Hell, no!"

"Alright. I know it's not going to be easy at first, Ki Ki, but nothing worth working for truly is. We've got enough saved to get by, so we'll manage." Gerald caressed his wife's shoulders. "Damn, Ki Ki, you so tense."

"I can't help it. You know how I – "

"Shhh. Just let all those worries go. Everything's gonna be just fine," Gerald paused, holding her body tight and snug. He leaned forward and kissed her cheek. "Besides, six months from now, if push comes to shove and you haven't gotten your first paycheck, then guess what?"

"What?"

"Your ass is getting a job at Mickey D's."

Kiana giggled and struggled to free her arms to slap Gerald upside his head, but couldn't do so. She smiled in admiration of her husband's optimism. That was one of his enduring qualities that she adored about him. He had always been supportive of her desire to venture into real estate from the first day she enrolled in The Real Estate Institute at Temple University's Center City Campus last September to pursue a full time career as a real estate salesperson.

He rested his chin on Kiana's shoulder. "Can you do me a favor?"

"Anything."

"I want you to close your eyes and relax."

Kiana sucked her teeth and smirked. "Okay."

Gerald began stroking Kiana's breasts. She turned her head clockwise to the steady pace of his fingertips tracing the perimeter of her nipples. He leaned forward and began sucking on her shoulder blade.

"Mmmm," Kiana whispered, extending her right arm to caress the back of his head. She purred and nestled her body against Gerald's when she heard the introduction of Robin Thicke's *Lost Without You* exude from the radio.

"Looks like somebody's feeling better," Gerald said.

She opened her eyes. "I love this song. It reminds me of how you make me feel."

"And how's that?"

She turned around and rested on her knees. Wrapping her arms around Gerald's chest, she leaned forward and whispered, "You make me feel loved."

"Oh yeah?"

"Mm hmmm," she nodded and kissed her husband.

Kiana leaned back and released the stopper in the bathtub. She stood up, picked up her shower cap on the caddy and covered her hair. Gerald stood up and started picking rose petals from his skin. He watched his wife turn on the faucets to activate the shower. Drawing the shower curtain to keep the

27

water inside, , Kiana walked towards her husband and kissed his pecs. Her tongue slithered across the epidermal landscapes of his abdominals and into his pubic hairs until she began sucking his dick.

"Ooh, Ki Ki," Gerald moaned and hissed.

Pressing her thumbs into his oblique muscles, she kneaded her fingernails into the small of his back. As the pulsating stream of water sprayed across their bodies, his hands gently caressed her shoulders and began their ascension towards her shower cap.

Kiana pulled back, stood up and adjusted her cap. "Don't get my hair wet or I'll kill you!"

"Chill, honey, I got this," he answered, switching places with his wife.

Positioning her body around to face the cream-colored tile wall, Gerald rocked his wife gently from left to right to the shower's rhythm. The strength of his bulging biceps and forearms made Kiana feel ecstatic, but that was nothing compared to his next move. His fingers slowly crept their way across the contour of her hips and pelvis, plucking rose petals from her body until they danced their way into her vagina. She moaned and screamed in delight as he massaged throughout her erogenous zones while come permeated from her sweet spot.

"Does that feel good to you?" he asked, whispering in her ear.

"Hell, yeah!" she screamed, slapping the tile with her hands.

He turned Kiana to face him, lifted her into the air and pressed her against the wall. He inserted his hard dick between her legs as their lips locked in another passionate kiss. Pounding her heels into the tub, he dug deeper into her body and soul with his thickness. She could feel Gerald's heartbeat against her breast while he slowly gyrated back and forth. Her body felt warm and hot with every minute that passed.

"Fuck it!" Kiana yelled, tossing her shower cap into the tub.

Gerald's eyes bulged and he stared at her with his mouth agape. She knew firsthand that it would be a matter of moments before his bottom lip would tremble and he would explode. Sure enough, she was right on the money and on perfect sync as they climaxed in unison.

Kiana wrapped her arms around Gerald when he slid his dick from inside her and gently allowed her feet to touch the tub. She sank into the remnants of rose petals lying in the tub as he turned off the water and pulled back the shower curtain. Stepping out of the tub, Gerald reached for a towel and handed it to his wife.

Kiana stood up and covered her body. "Thanks, baby," she said, sitting on the edge of the tub.

"No problem," he replied, catching his breath.

Gerald sat down on the toilet seat, picked up a slice of mango and offered some to Kiana. She smiled, took a bite and stared seductively at her husband while chewing on the juicy pulp.

BILL HOLMES is an artist who has dared to dream in the face of adversity while recognizing the divine nature of life and its infinite possibilities. As a respected poet, writer and author on the Philadelphia spoken word scene, Bill has touched many souls through his creative endeavors by striving towards excellence in everything he does. His performances have captivated many audiences through his unique style of humor, insight, spirituality, pride, and most importantly, love and appreciation of a woman.

By no means is Bill afraid "to keep it real when expressing the importance of self-love." He is also the author of the ESSENCE best-selling fiction novel, *One Love*, the full-length poetry book *Straight From My Heart*, and the spoken word CD, *The Air I Breathe*. Bill has been featured and has performed at various poetry venues from Philadelphia to Washington, DC, opening for artists such as the Last Poets and award-winning jazz musician Roy Ayers. His work has been published and featured in the *Philadelphia Tribune*, ESSENCE Magazine, and the anthology *Journey Into My Brother's Soul*. He is also a contributing writer and poet for the forthcoming anthologies *Step Up To The Mic: A Poetic Explosion* and *Triumph of My Soul*.

Vengeance

Watching through the mirrored glass as Black Widow spread her long slender dark chocolate legs, sent a chill up my spine. Slowly she opened her thighs laughing as she gently teased her slave. Her body was a perfect size ten frame. My senses tensed as my eyes gazed over the soft curves that hugged her body tightly. Smiling at Black Widow's attempt to suppress her desire for him, forced the blood in my body to flow only where it was needed. In the dark midnight corner of the bedroom, I could see his muscle-bound frame slither closer and closer to his destination. A sensual chill slithered down my spine as he placed his face inside her warm soft thighs.

The sight of Black Widow's hips dancing to the rhythm of her dark lover's head caused her to moan loud enough for me to hear her faint whimpers through the thick-mirrored glass. It was at that moment, I craved her. My desire to feel the gratifying torment of those full thick lips, sucking out the uncontrollable throbbing caused a huge bulge to protrude through my sweatpants. Black Widow overpowered my reason. I wanted to be inside her, but my craving to watch her was my poison.

I couldn't take the pleasurable pain as I watched him crawl up to her face, kissing her curves tenderly. My mouth watered at the sight of her licking her own juices off his lips. Everything moved in slow motion while his body penetrated my wife, his hips thrust deeper and deeper inside her sweet nectar. At that moment I was hooked, I wanted more. From then on, my wife and I became the exclusive members on the elite sex club Vengeance. I was no longer Devin, my wife was no longer Karma. I was now Eros and she, was my Black Widow.

Vengeance saved our marriage in a way. The club gave us a way out of our boring little existence. I was bored and Karma was ready to divorce me and move on to something better. Our trouble started when we discovered that it was going to be difficult for Karma to have children. Before that night, our sex life was my addiction. The very thought of being inside of Karma's warm tight walls would almost make me bust through my pants.

Karma would let me do just about anything to her body that pleased me. The best sex we had was the night I made her my slave. Karma had come home to our one bedroom apartment after working all day. The apartment was surrounded by darkness as her shadow graced the illuminating walls.

"Devin, baby, are you home yet. I'm tired. I had a really rough day." In the silent shadows I waited for her, contemplating my next move. "Devin, where are you?" Hearing the desperation in her voice added to my excitement. I could tell she was getting angry. "Devin, where the fuck are you, the apartment isn't that big. If you're in here with another bitch, you know what I will do." The sex was always better when she was enraged.

Creeping up behind her, my fingers slithered over her firm waist pulling her close to my body as we stumbled back on the night stand. Grabbing a handful of her thick auburn hair, she let out a moan. Breathing deeply she begged, "Tell me how you want it."

Smiling, I whispered softly in her lovely ears, "You know. Now *bend over*."

Obeying my command, Karma walked over to the bed and, bending her round plump ass over, she spread her juicy lips open for me to taste her sweet nectar from behind. My mouth watered as I remembered the last time my tongue was blessed with her warm juices coating my throat.

The pussy was always tight and that night was no exception. Feeling her clit grow as my fingers slipped over the silky flesh that held her sexual sensitivity, made her quiver in my arms. I almost came when the head of my dick kissed the lining of her moist lips. Drilling a dent in my wife's warm ocean was my main concern for the night. Bending down so that she could hold her ankles, Karma spread her swollen lips wide open for me as I forced her walls to submit to me.

Her legs began to shake violently when the head of my dick encircled the lining of moisture, only to slowly bathe in her wetness. Feeling her warm juices drip down the shaft of my dick, I heard her laugh. Tauntingly she asked, "Is that all you have?" The haunting laughter of my wife's seductive voice made my dick rock hard. Her laughter turned into moans of pleasure as her hips slammed wildly into mine, as she begged me for more. "Harder, baby. Please." Suddenly I saw a new toy sitting quietly up against the corner. Karma sensed why I stopped when she looked over at the corner wall. Walking over she pulled the rocking chair out of the corner so that she could hold onto the back of the chair. Smiling I pulled her hips closer to mine.

Gripping her hair tighter, my hips pounded against her plump ass. Sounds of our skin slapping each other became the soundtrack for our lust. Fucking her from behind, Karma held on tight to the back of the rocking chair. As the chair met our rocking motions, I decided to try a new position. Pushing her upper body forward so that her 36C's hung over the chair, she spread her legs wider, allowing me to stretch her legs out so that I was able to put her in a spread eagle position while I fucked her from behind. Standing on the back of the chair our hips locked in a powerful grip.

"Oh baby. That's the spot. Right there. Hold it!"

Karma submitted to my will; I continued to go deeper and deeper each time she swung back on my hips. My dick gushed inside of her body refusing to leave. Soaking in a sinful bliss, Karma whispered, "Let me please you, Master. I want to taste you."

Doing as she requested I pulled out of the warmest place on earth, only to feel the warmth of her tongue wrap around the head of my throbbing dick. She made sure her lips softly grazed my balls each time she took the head of my dick deeper down her throat.

This was how our sex life used to be, before work started and marriage made sex boring. The thrill that we used to have was long gone. We went from having sex two to three times a day to once a week maybe. Even when we were having sex it was the same position—missionary or doggy. Nothing new, or exciting, that is until I found out about the elite sex club, Vengeance. You see, it all started in the summer. We had been married for four years and our spark was gone.

Karma was a secretary working for a financial consultant firm, and I was in law school and waiting for a job position at a wealthy law firm that I had just applied for. Money was never enough, and with school to add to the bills, every dime we made went back to Uncle Sam before we could even touch it. One of my classmates jokingly told me about this club that requires you to take a little blue pill before you enter the club. They had rules and if you got passed the steel doors, you *wanted* to be initiated.

"Devin, you have to take Karma with you. This place allows you to let go of your sexual fears. They associate your deepest fear with your wildest fantasy. The entrance to the palace is two steel doors. When you enter the club, you step through a water fountain they say is used to cleanse you from the outside world. But before leaving, you have to go through the same water fountain to cleanse yourself of their world as well. Once you go through the purification, you are greeted by a waiter or waitress from your dreams."

Taking him for a joke, I laughed. "Yea okay, so what kind of women are there? Is this one of your imaginary cases where the man is accused of joining an orgy?"

Laughing Trevon replied, "Nope. This place is official. You're greeted with the sounds of women moaning while other beautiful women suck on any part of their bodies. The host is said to be the most beautiful woman in the club. She stands at five-feet-inch inches tall, with her butter smooth complexion. Her ice blue eyes taunt your soul as her body seduces your flesh. One whisper from her luscious full lips makes the atmosphere complete. You will want to have anyone of her slaves wrap their lips around your dick. Just to slide a finger in that sweet pussy would make any man cry."

"Where is this place and how do you know so much about it?"

Laughing, Trevon opened his Newport cigarettes as he pounded the pack into his fists. "I was told as I'm telling you now."

"So that's how you get in? Is this like *Eyes Wide Shut*? Will everyone be in masks?"

Trevon grabbed my arm as he pulled me closer to his silver Lexis SUV. Handing me a card he said, "Go on this web site tonight. The screen will say that it has expired but don't worry.

That's how they discreetly trace you. About two or maybe three days later you will receive an invitation for you and one guest. Take Karma with you. They let you watch or they can watch you."

Smiling I took the card, sliding it into my pocket I waived Trevon goodbye. On the way home, I thought about what Karma would say. She used to be down for me in whatever I wanted. *She would want this more than me,* I thought as I slid the card back inside my pocket.

๛ ๛ ๛ ๛ ๛

"Baby, could we talk for a sec?"

Looking up from her book, Karma soaked her pleasurable lips inside mine as she kissed me seductively on the lips. As our lips parted she smiled, "What's up baby?"

Stunned I pulled her closer to me. "Let's play a game, Master and Slave." Before she could answer me I pulled her body close to mine. Kissing her softly as I allowed my lips to graze her flesh, my fingers slid under the covers anticipating having to remove her pajama bottoms. My hand met with the soft curly hairs that covered those plump lips. Spreading her lips open my fingers danced in her wetness.

"I heard about this sex club called Vengeance. They have slaves who tend to your every need. They turn your biggest fear into your wildest fantasy."

Moaning, while my fingers became reacquainted with her G-spot, she agreed. "Anything you want, Master," she cooed with pleasure.

Arriving at Vengeance, we were greeted with marble columns that touched the diamond lit sky. As the heavy silver metal doors opened, we slipped into the darkness and greeted by a beautiful five-foot-ten-inch butter cream goddess. Her hair was shoulder length and jet black. Walking into the room, the candlelight exposed her bluish sliver eyes. Her dress was black with a low cut back; hugging every curve she possessed as if she were a very valuable prize. Her skin was the mixture of a milk almond flowing over her body. My mouth salivated from the thought of sucking on her melon-sized breasts. She was beautiful, and noticing my obvious stares, she smiled.

The male slave who stood beside the host of the club entranced my wife. He was dark chocolate and full of probably steroid filled muscles. His eyes were a deep black that would pull any female in if she wasn't careful. I could tell he wanted her, and so could the host.

"Hello, my name is Chaos and I am your host for as long as you desire." Walking up to us, Chaos pressed her body close to mine so that her nipples grazed my shirt. Her slave grabbed my wife, pushing his tongue inside her mouth. In a heated gaze Chaos pulled my lips to hers while she distracted me from my wife's newfound pleasure. The taste of her lips left a poisonous vibe that tainted my soul.

Her kisses intensified while my wife's footsteps grew into a quiet whisper that trailed off into the dark atmosphere. Tilting her head to the right, her luscious lips open slightly, allowing a warm fluid to glide down my throat. Little did I know that she had just fed me liquid X through the champagne she allowed to slip inside my mouth. Her sultry voice floated around the room as Chaos pulled my hand, forcing my body to walk with hers. With just one look her slave took my wife into the darkness of the club. In a hypnotizing whisper I heard, "Tell me your fantasy. What pleases you the most?"

Her beauty mesmerized my body, causing my heart to pound harder at the thought of my dick swimming inside her body. The thought of her walls slowly stretching to conform to my body ran through my mind as she stared into my eyes. "I bet it's a submissive woman. Someone who will let you tie them up anyway you want. Someone you can have your way with all the time. Is that what you want Devin."

Biting my lip, I tried to suppress the pleasure I felt when her voice whispered my name. Pulling me into a hidden room, we waited. Hidden behind a mirror, I saw Karma walk blindfolded into the room. Guided by Chaos' slave she sat down nervously on the bed. Her new lover waited in the darkness, watching his prey, anticipating the time she would yield to him. My eyes burned as she waited for him. Chaos waited as she crept down onto the floor, covering the head of my dick with her sweet lips, I exhaled.

Her muscles created a suction forcing me to slide down her throat with ease. As my wife's oral fixation was pleased over and over again, my pleasure was intensifying. Swelling inside her throat, I couldn't control myself. The urge to release my inhibitions deep inside her throat possessed me. This is how I watched my wife as she was flipped in every position for *her* new slave.

We drove home in a blanket of silence, neither one of us was really able to process what had just happened. Our next invitation came with our new names, Eros and Black Widow. Love meets danger. Two days later I received a call from a wealthy Law Firm, asking me to come in for an interview. Walking into the office, I was greeted by my potential boss.

"Hello, *Eros*. Remember me."

My Chaos had just begun.

NYAH STORM is the best-selling author of *Confessions of a Sex Therapist* and a native of Washington, D.C., with a B.S. in Psychology, which gives her erotic novels a psychological twist. A writer since childhood, Nyah honed her writing skills through her poetry. When Nyah is not writing, she is curled up in a corner with a book or chilling out to music.

ELISSA GABRIELLE

Chocolate Dreamin'

T he next poet, to grace our stage, is a sister who really needs no introduction. Please, welcome back, the very gracious and sexy, Nina Reign," Ali says as he extends his arms to greet me, taking my hand into his, escorting me to the stage of The Hype, a hot poetry venue in the heart of downtown Newark. I flawlessly flow to the mic, acknowledging the band behind me with a brief nod of the head and, of course, a sexy smile. The dim lights and candles lit all around sets the tone in the club, making it one of intrigue, sexiness and passion. The amber spotlight finally arrives at the center of my caramel-coated lips, and I imagine it offsets my wavy, shoulder-length, dark brown hair. I feel sexy, and everyone in the house is about to find out. I hope Nasir gets the point, takes heed to my message, feels my rhythm and gives in to my unspoken carnal requests.

Gently caressing the mic and its bulbous head, as if it is Nasir, I begin to spill it—my heart that is. My desires, for all in this little private world to hear, especially him, whom I can't seem to let escape my naughty fantasies, in my mind anyway, will have its story told this evening. This is way beyond infatuation. I yearn for him to justify my lust.

"Thank you. Peace and blessings family. It's been a minute. I want to bless you with this piece called *Them There Eyes*. I'm

40

just going to spit from the dome. I hope you enjoy." Here we go. Exhaling first and getting a slight wind in my hips, I move to the beat of the drummer.

"Windows to your soul
had me trippin'
as if Coltrane was tickling the back of my neck
while Gil was reciting
and Jill was mesmerizing
and Badu was electrifying
chills went thru my thighs
as I gazed starry-eyed into them there eyes.

It was as enchanting as a drink with Common
and then a one-night stand
and as picture perfect as a
private show from Dizzy Gillespie's Band
like Angelou discovered why I was singing
and Morrison gave me Paradise.
and the warmth found a place between my thighs
soul-searching into them there eyes.

And I blinked and saw you there
talk that shit to me Papi
so magical, and so lovely
my warmth turned to heat
and my nipples got a rise
your eyes

I blink, and I blink, and I blink
yet I cannot breakout from this zone
that I am overjoyed to be cruisin' in

Can you feel the heat?
my temperature is sky high
and I blink one more time
and I see your nature rise
I lick my lips and blink again
and you slowly come inside.
your eyes

and while you are
Stroking...
my intellect
and moistening me
with...
your vernacular
my initial instinct
is to...
throw it on ya

Eyes Almighty
I implore – permeate and resonate your exuberant wisdom
all over me, into me
and don't get it twisted
I am superable
you are Supreme
paramount
and I blink one last time
realizing that it is evident that you can't be touched
rain your shine down on me
and look at me one more time
your eyes."

The standing "O" makes me blush as Ali smiles, claps and escorts me off the stage. Finally reaching the bar, I meet up with my girl Destiny who is all aglow. "Girl, why don't you just tell the boy how you feel?" she jokes as I get comfortable on the bar stool.

"No dear, I can't bring myself to say a word. And shut up anyway, because you're the only one who knows," I respond while signaling for the bartender to come over. "I'll have a Cosmopolitan, thanks."

A tap on my shoulder abruptly interrupts my intimate moment with the Cosmopolitan that was just served and I turn around to see who it is. "I loved that piece you performed a minute ago," he says, grinning from ear to ear, extending his hand to shake mine. "My name is Paul. Nice to meet you." I smile and just as I'm about to introduce myself for the sake of courtesy, Ali's voice immediately traps me into tunnel vision.

"Alright, beautiful people. Coming to the stage is Nasir."

Incredibly rude, I become instantaneously as I ask Paul, Peter, whatever his name is to please, "Excuse me," as I spin my barstool around to catch the perfect view of all that is perfect and fine and delicious; Nasir. He deliciously parts his lips to speak and in doing so, sets a ten-alarm fire to the fragrant walls of my sex. The sexiness in his grin, makes me eager, anxious to grab hold of anything he'll offer, for dear life. He's delectable in a crisp baby blue button-up, loose fitting Parishrformel jeans in navy, and a perfectly trimmed goatee that has the power to make me instantly drop to my knees and begin sucking on cue, if I had to; if only for one night. His deep set, dark brown eyes are staring only at me, and his shiny bald head is polished to perfection. Damn, he is glorious and damn it I'm all ears.

"Peace, everyone. I call this piece, *Chocolate Dreamin'*." He points in my direction, repositions the mic and speaks, to what seems to be directed at me.

Initially our eyes met briefly and implored for the chance
to welcome heavy breathing,
hunger,
needing.
May I kiss the brown flesh and begin eating?
I beg you to discard all your uncertainties,
and we'll wet together
as the taste of your sweet skin between my lips
ignites and intoxicates
then our heated tongues will meet in the midst
of hot and quickening breath
as I fill you up with all I have left
saturating you with me
dance to my rhythm baby
you can have all you want
if you just ask
Do you want me?
Let me take you from a whisper to a scream
While chocolate dreamin'

Seems as though everyone in the club knows something I don't, or at least won't admit. "He wants you Nina," Destiny says as Nasir stares at me as he walks off the stage. We've been playing this game too long. If I don't have this man soon, I'm going to explode.

"Come on, Destiny, let's get out of here," I say to her knowing damn well I see him heading in my direction. Shit. What am I to say? Well, think quickly, he's here.

"Nice piece," I say, devouring him with my eyes. If he only knew the shit I want to do to him.

"Thanks. I loved your piece as well," Nasir tells me looking even more delicious up close. Damn, I want to suck his dick in the worst way. Reaching into his pocket, he pulls out his card and hands it to me. "Give me a call tonight, if you don't have any plans."

"Thanks, I sure will Nasir."

The erotic kiss he plants on my cheek sends a chill up my spine, down my right thigh, up my left, straight to my nipples and lands on my clit, where it is now throbbing profusely. The look of passion on his face is about as subtle as the size of my breasts, and trust me, I'm giving him cleavage for days. *Hot damn.*

"So, are you going to call him?"

"Yes, Destiny, I will call. But, not tonight. I don't want him to think I'm desperate."

"Desperate? Are you serious? The two of you have been making love to one another for two weeks now up there on that stage! Gimme a break! Call that boy!"

"I'm scared."

"Grow up, bitch, and call him. I say that with lots of love."

We both laugh. A few more poets grace the stage and we head out. Both of us have work in the morning.

ఆ ఆ ఆ ఆ ఆ

As I toss and turn in this bed, I can't help but imagine what Nasir is doing. The violet-colored chemise caresses my curves in all the right places, and the silk brushes against my nipples, turning me on even more. Could it be the bedroom attire turning me on this way? Absolutely not. It's Nasir. Should I call him? Nah. Maybe tomorrow. Taking another glance at my alarm clock, I realize it's time to get some sleep. Early morning tomorrow for me as the children in my class have state exams, so it'll be test packets and number two pencils all day. Okay, now its midnight and I must get some sleep. Off goes the repeat of *Law and Order.*

The light from the half moon peers ever so slightly through the bedroom window, making it easy for me to see my nipples rising. My fantasies kick into overdrive. Did he say, "chocolate dreaming?" Yes, I'm chocolate dreaming to the tenth power, at twelve-thirty a.m., where now my pillow attempts to extinguish the roaring flames between my thighs, and its soft, plush edge rests against my bulging clit, pulsating in anticipation of him.

My phone rings.

"Hello?"

"Hi, Nina. Did I wake you?"

"No, I'm trying to get to sleep, not there yet. Who's calling?"

"How many men do you have calling at midnight?"

"None, which is the reason I asked."

"Nina, its Nasir. I'm sorry to bother you so late."

"It's no bother, but how did you get my number?"

"Your friend Destiny gave it to me."

"Oh, I see."

"You see what, Nina?"

"Nothing."

"So, is it a bad time?"

"Not at all. I can't get to sleep."

"Me either."

"And why is that, Nasir? Maybe you need to drink some hot tea or take something to soothe you."

"That could be true, or…"

"Or, what?"

"Maybe I can drink you. That will soothe me."

"Is that right?"

"Yes."

"Mmm, well, we'll have to arrange that."

"I'm yours for the taking, Nina."

"I'm flattered, Nasir."

"So Nina, what are you wearing?"

"A purple nighty."

"Do you have panties on?"

"No, Nasir. I don't."

"Mmmm."

"Mmmm, what?"

"Just sounds so good to me."

"Why is that?"

"I can just imagine tasting you. You look so good and if you look good, you must taste good."

"Mmmm, Nasir, I have to go."

"Why, Nina? I know you're feeling me. When you get on that stage you're speaking to me, right?"

"Right."

"So speak to me now."

"I can't right now. You caught me at an awkward moment."

"Why is that?"

"I was just thinking of you, Nasir."

"Oh yeah?"

"Yeah."

"I want you, Nina."

"I want you too, Nasir."

"Can I have you now?"

"You can't come over this late, Nasir."

"Put your phone on speaker."

"Why?"

"Just do it, baby, for me…please."

"Okay, it's on speaker."

"Take off your clothes."

"My chemise is off."

"Lay on your back, baby," Nasir commands.

"Now, bend your knees."

"Nina, spread your legs, nice and wide, for me."

Silence.

"Just imagine me there with you, Nina, and my lips kissing you softly all over your beautiful body. Can you imagine that, Nina?"

"Yes, I can, Nasir."

"Now, picture my tongue gliding over your nipples, and then I suck them, real slow and long. Rub your nipples for me, Nina. Get them hard for me."

"Mmmm. Nasir, I can't do this. Mmmmm."

"Put your tongue on your nipples and think of me."

"Mmmm."

"Do you like the way I feel, Nina?"

"Yes."

"Now, take your hands and rub your thighs. Spread your legs, gorgeous. Suck your fingers and start rubbing my clit, Nina. It's mine, right?"

"Yes, Nasir."

"Rub it nice and slow, then stick your fingers in all that sweetness for me. Pull it out then in, over and over again, as if I'm inside you real deep."

"Mmmm, Nasir."

"Oh baby, I'm almost there, Nina. Shit, I'm coming now. Oooh, damn. I can't wait to get my hands on you girl."

"I'm there too, Nasir. Oh God, mmmm, this feels so good."

"I'm going to make you feel even better tomorrow, Nina. I'll meet you at the club."

"Okay, bye baby."
"Bye sweetheart."

❧ ❧ ❧ ❧ ❧

"Blessing us again, y'all, is Ms. Nina Reign. Show her some love." Ali, once again, welcomes me to the stage.

"Hello, again, good people. I call this one *Get Lifted*. Enjoy."

I wanna be your diva
Your secret keeper
Dream weaver
Jism releaser
Pleasure seeker
My treat, it's on me.

I'm beggin' to spread
My yearnin' all across your head
And then eat it.
Hungry,
Like a new boxer.
Driven,
to be your provider.

I know it's crazy
But my smile is somewhere off,
Far gone
In a distant
Galaxy
Until
I hear my name-
Part so deliciously

49

From your lips
To my ears.

Do feed me,
Then fuck me,
Like Mos.
Hold me,
Want me,
Let's get lifted,
Like Legend.
Spank, wind and bend,
To get dem juices flowin'
Over and over again.

Snap, crackle and pop me
From here,
There
everywhere
To infinity.

But wait,
Don't love me
Then leave me
As the thought of having you once
Only
Would ache my heart strings
Can I really have you, baby?

Ali walks me off the stage, and I head towards the ladies room, before joining Destiny at the bar. I didn't see Nasir this evening, which sends my emotions into a tailspin. It's all good. I walk down the three steps leading to the lower level ladies room, knock on the door, no one is occupying it, so I head in, turn around to lock it when my heart races and the yearning between my sugar walls is at an all time high.

"Hello, Beautiful."

"Hi, Nasir. I didn't see you earlier."

"I was in the back. I heard your piece. Was that for me?"

"Maybe."

"Yeah?"

His seductive smile melts my insides and brings out the devil in me.

"It could've been for you."

Licking his lips, Nasir slowly approaches. I back up to create much needed space between us.

"Nasir, this is a ladies bathroom, honey, you have to get out now."

Nasir joins me in the bathroom, locks the door behind him, moves in so close to me, invading all my space, backs me up to the sink; I have no choice but to sit there. Opening my mouth with his thumb, he parts my lips and kisses them, placing his tongue in my mouth, licks my lips and moans.

"Damn, Nina, I've been dying to taste those pretty lips for so long."

His strong, big hands open my blouse to where he finds full breasts awaiting. He leans in and begins sucking, cupping both breasts into his powerful hands, outlining my nipples with his tongue, sucking with so much purpose.

"Mmmm, Nina, I love your Tootsie Roll nipples. You taste as good as I imagine. Can I have you now, baby?"

"Yes, Nasir."

Nasir takes off his shirt to reveal bold and beautiful brown skin, while I pull off my blouse and skirt. His pants fall, but don't hit the floor before my panties do.

"Squat over my face, Nina."

I oblige.

"Mmm, your pussy tastes good Nina."

Sweet, light flickers of his tongue, guide my every grind on his face. With each lick, he becomes more bold, daring, and the light, polite touch of his tongue, now turns into intrepid, deep, wet, wide, determined brush strokes, making me shiver in pleasure and moan in pure ecstasy.

If I pull his face any further into my love, it'll look like I gave birth to him.

"Nasir, please hurry, please…fuck me."

Nasir seductively looks up at me with a glazed euphoria in his eyes; the look you get when you want to fuck someone so bad. Getting up, Nasir lifts and props me up onto the bathroom sink, and commands, "Spread that pussy real nasty for me, Nina. Let me see it."

I oblige.

"Mmm, it looks so good baby; it's so pretty. Do you want me now, Nina?"

"Yes, Nasir, please."

As he pulls out that sweet brown pipe, my initial reaction is to suck it, but I can't move from this position I'm in. I want him so bad. I need to feel him right now. As I begin pulling him closer to me, kissing his lips, I can smell my pussy on his breath, turning me on like crazy. Grabbing the mouth-watering embellishment, rubbing my clit with the tip vigorously, makes me a hot wet mess, as all of my juices swirl around from the head of his magic to the walls of my wonderment, Nasir has got me so ripe and ready. He's ready. Yet, he's fucking with me.

"Tell me you want me, Nina."

"I do, Nasir, so fucking bad. Please let me have it now."

"Kiss me, Nina."

The fervent kiss I plant on his caramelized lips comes with an eternity of lust behind it. Breathing is erratic, heavy and heated.

Nasir lifts my leg and inserts deeply with conviction as I cry out in ecstasy. The length of his manhood fills me up so quickly, so well; it's everything I imagined and more. His powerful thrusts in and out of me makes my pussy walls give way to every one of his dominant blows as the sopping sounds of sweet, slick, sex saturate the bathroom, as well as all of my senses. The motions in and out, round and round, side to side drives me nuts; I'm going to bust. Mmm, look at him, licking my tits, smacking my ass, talking all the good shit I love to hear.

"Damn, Nina, you feel so fucking good, baby. Mmm, I can't hold on too much longer."

A sensual rage consumes me, and the fire in my eyes confirms, as much as he better not take this dick away from me so soon, for I am insatiable. "Please, Nasir, don't cum yet. Please don't take it away from me."

"I'm trying Nina, it's so good."

"Pull it out Nasir, so you can relax a bit."

"I can't, Nina. I'll slow down," Nasir confesses, as the heat pours from his lips onto mine.

"Oooh shit, Nasir, damn…oh God…I'm cumming…shit… Nasir…you so good…Mmmm."

"That's a good girl, cum all over me, baby. I have wanted you to release all over me for so long baby."

Glancing down at Nasir's dick, now in steel bat status, saturated with my nectar, as it goes in and out of all my goodness, creates a roaring flame, setting fire to my sugar walls again; ejaculation is inevitable, as heavy cream rises to the top.

Nasir rubs my clit as I explode all over him and he is now fucking me so slow and hard, pulling all the way out and going

53

back in with so much determination and passion, he's so nasty and greedy and damn, here we go again.

"Nasir, I can't take anymore...shit...you're making me cum again...oh God, please...ooh it's so good...Mmm...baby...Oh."

"Nina, I can't hold on any longer. Ahhhh."

Pulling out, the visual of a shiny, delicious and erect dick, fills Nasir's hand, as he jerks and strokes it, emptying its gratifying remains. The vanilla shake releasing all over the fine hairs of my sex is appetizing, inviting and satisfying and I'm wholly fulfilled; deliciously pleased.

Heavy panting, accompanied by a rewarded smile, Nasir thoroughly enjoyed himself.

"Was it good for you, Nina?"

"Oh yes, Nasir. You are so good," I respond, out of breath, and a hot, wet mess.

"Can I see you after this, Nina?"

"I'd have it no other way, baby."

Dubbed the "Queen of Hip Hop Romance Erotica" by *Disilgold Soul Magazine*, **ELISSA GABRIELLE** is the author of two poetry books, *Stand and Be Counted* and *Peace in the Storm*, and the highly-acclaimed novel *Good to the Last Drop,* and the sequel *Point of No Return* (August 2007), as well as the much anticipated novel *A Whisper to a Scream* (Christmas 2007). She is the founder of the greeting card line, Greetings from the Soul: The Elissa Gabrielle Collection. Gabrielle has graced the covers of *Conversations Magazine, Big Time Publishing Magazine,* and *Disilgold Soul Magazine.* Visit the author at www.elissagabrielle.com.

CREAM

A Room With A View

She smiled sweetly at her husband as she grabbed her purse and leaned in to kiss him softly on the cheek. He offered his freshly shaven cheek up for her kiss, and returned her smile with one of his own. She knew what was about to happen, and she was getting wet just thinking about it. Her car keys sat right on top of the junk in her purse, as if they were waiting for her to grab them. As she eased into her car and drove off, her face glowed with the secret knowledge that only she knew, that only she was privy to. She turned right at the corner of her sleepy subdivision block and parked a few feet from the corner, making sure that he couldn't see her car from their beautifully lit house. Just like clockwork, he ran out of the front door and made a beeline straight across the street to their neighbor's house, the sexy new neighbor who'd just moved in about two months ago. The young woman opened the door and kissed him sweetly as he gently pushed her back inside, carefully looking around to see if anyone was observing them. Someone was. *She* was, his wife of almost eighteen years, the mother of his three children, the lover who'd shared his bed until recently. She'd gotten out of her car and hid in the tall bushes at the corner so that he couldn't see her watching him enjoy this other woman more than she had been enjoying him of late.

Something had happened that neither one of them could put their finger on, but the fire of desire between them had become a cold, sooty ember. She hurriedly got back in her car and drove around the block, quietly pulling back into her garage as if she'd never left. He thought she'd be gone to her yoga class, which usually lasted about an hour and a half. You know what they say—when the cat's away, the mice will play, and this rat was planning on getting busy very quickly.

She ran upstairs to their tastefully decorated bedroom and stripped off all her clothes, leaving them in a pile on the beautiful hardwood floor. Very uncharacteristic of her, a known neat freak. But right now, time was of the essence if she was to catch the view. She bolted from their bedroom to their oldest son's junky room, which had a window that faced directly across the street from the new neighbor's house. Keeping the lights off, she managed to find the high-powered telescope they had gifted their son for his thirteenth birthday four months ago.

She was the one who taught him how to use it since his dad never seemed to have the time or the interest. Always working, no time for a life. No time for their children, and no time for her, either. Everything was about making money to get out of the hole. She secretly resented him for abandoning her like that, but needed for the children to have the benefits of having both parents in their lives—what little that amounted to. She was learning to do without him, although she did sometimes miss the intimacy they used to share. Now there was a different type of interest. She pointed the telescope toward the new neighbor's dimly lit upstairs bedroom. Will wonders never cease? She was amazed at how powerful this telescope truly was. She could see almost everything going on in that bedroom, as if she was standing right inside it. There he was, her husband, standing there, trying to look sexy with his rock-hard dick in his hand, stroking it slowly as the new neighbor watched from the foot of her king-sized bed. He didn't look half-bad for fifty-five, but he was not in the neighbor's league at all. She was every bit of twenty-eight and worked as a photo model for several major ad agencies. She was beautiful, absolutely beautiful. The wife, a very sexy fifty-four-year old with still-perky titties, wondered what the new neighbor saw in him, and figured that it might be just a sugar-daddy thing or the new neighbor was just horny and thought he was safe—since he had a wife and kids—and wouldn't be hounding her. Just another man out for a little extra on the side. But dogs come in all shapes, sizes and genders.

The new neighbor pulled him right in front of her as she sat on the bed and proceeded to take his big dick into her pretty mouth with a move that even Deep Throat would've been proud of. She didn't choke or gag, but just let it slide down her throat until his nuts were juxtaposed against her chin. His head fell back as his wife watched through the telescope. She could feel the wetness building between her legs. She quickly spread her legs open and began to finger her clit. It was hard like a small pebble. She wanted to lie down on the bed and finish what she'd started, but she realized that she was not in her own room. She didn't want to leave any stains or the sweet smell of wet pussy in her son's room, so she stopped for a moment and went back to being a visual voyeur.

By the time she went back to check the view through the telescope, her husband and the sexy new neighbor were both naked and thoroughly engaged in some serious six-nine action. He was positioned on top of her with her beautiful, shapely brown legs spread wide open, as he used his long tongue to lick all around her sweet clit, sucking it ever so gently. The new neighbor was gyrating beneath him while still deep throating his massive dick. Her exquisite body was worthy of the cover of the best porn magazine in existence. The wife admired her husband's skills from afar, remembering that warm feeling that would engulf her when he used to do the same things to her. Her own clit was truly throbbing now, signaling that she was almost ready for the ultimate meltdown that was about to ensue. There was just one more visual she needed to see.

They had gone as far as they could with the oral sex, and now they were ready. Ready for him to enter her. He paused briefly to put on his condom and started to slide his big, long prick into her wet, waiting cunt. His wife had been waiting for this one moment. It was the moment that she had always enjoyed the most. She could almost feel it herself, from across the street. It always hurt a little at first, but then the tight pussy muscles would give way to the indescribably pleasurable feeling of being totally filled up inside. There used to be nothing like it. She pushed two fingers into her sopping wet pussy—she couldn't help herself—and kept the other hand on the telescope, determined not to miss anything. Her husband was fucking the shit out of the sexy new neighbor and they both loved it. Hot sweat was flying everywhere and their faces were linked together with locked tongues. He was pumping her cunt hard and she was taking every strong, solid inch of him. His wife was about to come as she continued to stare through the telescope. She quickly grabbed a towel out of her son's dirty clothes hamper and stuck it between her legs as she hollered out, "Freddie." As she came, she collapsed to the floor, tired and soaked in sweat, ready for some much-needed sleep. But she couldn't rest, for he'd be home shortly. She wiped her sweaty handprints off the telescope, threw the towel back in the hamper, made sure everything was just as she found it, quickly got dressed and ran down to her car in the garage. She slowly drove off around the corner to her hiding spot, only moments before spotting her husband creep back across the street, back into their house—what used to be their home.

As soon as she thought he'd been inside long enough, she pulled out her cell phone and dialed their number. When he answered, he tried to sound like she had awakened him from a deep sleep. She told him that the girls were going out for a bite to eat after yoga class and not to wait up for her. He was relieved that she wouldn't be home right away, because that would give him time to wash the sexy new neighbor's scent from his tired but satisfied body. He told her to take her time and be careful. She said she would and hung up quickly. With a big smile on her face, she hopped into her car and drove around the neighborhood for a couple of minutes. Long enough for her husband to have showered and changed his clothes. She pulled up to the house and clicked the garage door opener that she kept in her glove box. She eased her car quietly into the garage and jumped out with arms outstretched, running to the figure standing in the dimly lit doorway. They kissed passionately and tenderly embraced each other-one soft, voluptuous body pressed urgently against the other, as the wife uttered the same name again, "Freddie," the sexy new neighbor's name. Short for Fredricka.

The writer currently known as **CREAM** is a sweet, sexy African-American woman who is new to the writer's circle. *A Room with a View* is her first published short story. Cream writes poetry (erotic and general) and has written several other erotic stories that she hopes will be published some day, as well as being a talented singer/songwriter. She is divorced and resides in Southfield, Michigan.

Saltine or Ritz?

I t was Friday night and I was invited to a cabaret at Knights of Columbus in Forestville, Maryland. When my boys and I walked through the door, I immediate regretted making an appearance. And, having my partners with me made things even worse. The place was so dead, I thought I had seen Tupac. I guess white people aren't the only ones who see their dead icons. My buddies started clowning me bad because I said the party would be hot, saying they wanted their money back. That's when five of the finest women in the DC metropolitan area walked in the place. I had always seen ugly women traveling in packs but never fine ones. An exception to the rule, these women weren't just fine they were *foine*.

When the fellas spotted the young ladies, every last one of them changed their mind and wanted to stay. I had about three or four females coming through the party, so it didn't matter to me if we stayed or bounced. We found a table and sat down. Fifteen minutes later things changed. The Deejay played *Before I Let Go* by Frankie Beverly and Maze and the party was on and poppin'.

The Fab Five got up from their table and started dancing. The fellas decided to go over where they were and dance with them. Me, I laid back like I normally do with a cup of Remy Martin 1738 in one hand and a Corona in the other. I watched one of the Fab Five as she danced. This beautiful creature had movements that were fluid and sexy. Her hips swayed to the beat of the music as if she were an exotic dancer. I imagined her dancing on the pole in my bedroom. She would be my private dancer.

Then the Deejay did it, he played *Tiddy Balls* by the Junkyard Band. At that point, I couldn't hold it back any longer; I had to get my party on. When I hit the dance floor, the Remy had my head right. The melody of the music only increased my buzz and I felt just as high as a Georgia Pine. I started dancing and the Deejay put me in a DC state of mind. He played *The Water Dance* by the Northeast Groovers, *Cat in the Hat* by Lil Benny, *Body Snatchers* by Rare Essence and *Stormy Monday* by Chuck Brown. I was getting my groove on when I noticed one of the Fab Five sashaying her way towards me. She handed me a piece of paper with the name Renae and a phone number scribbled on it. By the time I had looked up, that fine beauty had walked away and was making her exit. The Fab Five had left the party.

Renae and I went out on four dates after that night. Hell, she came onto me and she was the one playing hard to get. She wouldn't even let a brotha hold her hand until the fourth date and that intrigued me. By date three, I would have already had sex with most of the women I dated. This was different for me. I was in unchartered territory. I needed to devise a plan to get back on track before our next encounter. I decided I needed to heat things up a bit. There wasn't a woman alive that could resist my charm when I was on my game.

We decided to get together one Thursday night to watch *Lackawanna Blues* on HBO. This was it. This was my time. The only place in the house where Renae had a television was in her bedroom and it was too big to move. I wore my black Shooters sweat suit, black Nike boots, and a splash of Creed Himalaya cologne. I'm not G. Garvin but I damn sure was going to turn up the heat.

Renae was wearing a white tank top, white boxer shorts and nothing else. I could see her delicious chocolate brown nipples through her shirt. Her five-foot-four-inch frame was toned and well put together. Her shoulder length hair was in a ponytail while her nails and feet were perfectly manicured.

I lay across the bed and started watching television. Renae slid into the bed and moved close to me. It felt as if Renae had turned up the heat when she began to rub her butt against my soldier or maybe it was just me getting hot. I kissed her on the back of her neck as I started caressing her thigh. I ran my hand up her thigh on the way to her tightly toned stomach making a brief stop at her sweet spot and played in her pubic hair. I kissed her shoulder and found my hand holding her breast.

It was hard to believe that Renae's tightly toned body was so soft. Being able to hold and caress such a beautiful woman had my dick as hard as Chinese arithmetic being done by a Russian in the dark. Renae rolled me over onto my back and straddled me like she was a jockey preparing to ride a Kentucky Derby winner. She lightly ran her fingernails up and down my chest as she grinded on my dick. I palmed her titties like I was giving her a breast exam. I watched as she threw her head back and her body started to quiver. It was time to unwrap my lollipop and start to take a lick and that's when it happened.

"Sweetie it's getting late and I think you should leave before something happens."

"Hunh!" I couldn't believe what I was hearing.

"You know I like you, but before we make love I have to make sure that you really want me."

"Do I really want you?" I grabbed my Johnson. "Girl, my dick don't get much harder than this. Hell yeah, I want you."

"Not like that boy. I need to know that you want me for me and not just for sex. I just want our first time to be special." She began to take off her shirt. "But if you want to do this right now then we can."

I stood there looking at her caramel breast with the chocolate nipples and wondered if this was a test. If it was a test I was destined to fail. I looked into her beautiful brown eyes, pulled her shirt down and said something I never thought I would hear myself say, "We can wait until you are ready." Then I went home and put an ice pack on my blue balls.

Well, tonight is finally the night that I get to taste Renae's sweet nectar. It has been six months since the encounter at Renae's home and I have been as dry as the Sahara Desert since the day I made my commitment to her. The only reason I hadn't cheated is because I am trying to do right by her. That really goes against my reputation as a ladies' man. I usually work with at least two women at a time. If one holds out, I would always have one on standby ready, willing, and able to satisfy my needs. My uncle once told me that it is a poor rat that only has one hole, and I lived by that code but things changed for me the night I met Renae.

The fellas would tease me about not getting any snooshie from Renae every chance they got. Whenever they would ask me had Renae given me any goodies, I would respond like Eddie Murphy in *Raw.* "Nope. She special, she think we should wait." The whole time I was hoping that she wasn't just a regular old cracker. I didn't think she was a plain cracker because of the way she handled herself on our first encounter. But hey, you never know. She could be like those fellas that are great street ball players but get them in a gym with referees and they're just average.

After that first night of borderline intimacy, I was on PR—panty restriction. Renae never told me that I was on PR but that is definitely what it was, a restriction. When she found out that I had gotten tickets for us to see Kem at Constitution Hall, she was ecstatic. When she saw that I didn't get just any seats but that I had called in some favors and got us seats—front row, center stage—the restriction was lifted.

Because I wanted this entire day to be filled with romance, I had yellow and white tulips delivered to Renae at work. The card that came along with the flowers was an invitation to the show that required her to RSVP. She responded to the RSVP request by emailing me some pictures of herself in some of the sexiest lingerie that I had ever seen with a note that read: *Yes, I will be attending this special event. On that evening, you will need to eat your Wheaties, put on your Hanes, and drink your Gatorade because I am going to need you to be a champ like Mike, and I don't mean Tyson or Jackson.*

After reading the email and seeing the pictures that Renae sent to me, I almost nutted all over myself. On Friday night, I was going to make sure that I was taking my ginseng and yohimbe. The one thing I didn't expect was Renae insisting on me driving my Crown Victoria instead of my Benz. She hated my Crown Vic but hey if that was what it was going to take for her to give me some punany, that's what I was going to do.

Raheem DeVaughn opened for Kem but I couldn't stay focused on the show because I was staring at Renae's ass all night. She didn't have a badonka donk but through her linen dress I could see that her butt was soft yet firm. Kem began to sing *It's a Matter of Time*. As Kem worked the audience with his sultry style, he walked down from the stage into the swaying crowd. Seeing Renae, singing every word of the song with him,

Kem leaned over and grabbed her hand as if he was singing to her. Then, he moved on throughout the crowd and Renae totally threw me off guard when she slid my hand up her thigh revealing to me that she didn't have any panties on. She moved my hand further up her dress and had me finger fuck her until she was dripping with moistness and almost at the brink of orgasm. I wanted to leave the concert when she began to suck on the two fingers that I had caressed her pussy with.

I touched, smelled, and tasted the prize that I had been coveting since the first day we met. I was so anxious about getting my prize that I could barely control myself on the drive home. A drive that was only twenty minutes seemed like it was taking forever. All Renae could talk about was Kem touching her hand and all I could think about was me playing with her pussy. Renae's hand was on my thigh the entire time caressing my manhood.

The closer we got to Renae's house, the harder my dick got. I could feel my heart pulsating in the shaft of my dick like it was about to burst. Renae had started to sing and as soon as I turned onto her street, she unbuckled my pants and began to use my dick as a microphone. That is when I realized why she wanted me to drive the Crown Vic. The Crown Vic doesn't have a center console, just one big seat.

As she slipped my dick into her mouth, her supple lips were so soft and moist that I found my eyes rolling into the back of my head several times. After all, my manhood hadn't felt like this in six months. I had to control myself from coming by thinking about something else because I wanted to lay it on her later. I wanted to get her hooked from the first taste, like a junkie on crack. Keep her coming back for more. If I worked it right, I would never have to wait another six months.

I drove five miles per hour to keep from crashing. When I finally pulled into her driveway Renae immediately stopped sucking my dick and ran into her home leaving the door open. With my rock hard dick in hand, I ran behind her hoping the night wasn't over.

I walked through Renae's front door to find her standing and waiting for me. She was already beautiful but she was absolutely breath taking by candlelight. The red La' Perla underwear and black Manolo Blahniks only added fuel to the fire that was burning within me.

Renae motioned for me to get undressed. I quickly took off my clothes, looking forward to the pleasure that I had been craving for the past six months. I stood staring at Renae just as naked as I was when I came into this world, hoping that she was going to finish what she had started.

Renae knelt down in front of me and slid a freshly sliced peach ring over my dick until it was at the back of my soldier. Then she began sucking on my dick while squeezing, rotating, and sliding the peach up and down my dick. As she nibbled on the peach, I could feel the juice from the peach running down. She sucked the juices into her mouth. She continued pleasuring me until I exploded from ecstasy.

Now, it was my turn to please her and I wanted her to regret ever making me wait so long for a taste of her love. I was going to suck on her pussy so long that she was going to have to beg me to return her ovaries.

Renae laid back and began to finger herself and I began to kiss on her thighs. Once she got her fingers nice and wet with her juices, I began to suck on them. Tonight, I was going to see how many licks it took to get to the center of the lollipop and that lollipop was Renae.

I got an ice cube from the glass bowl on the table and placed it on my tongue. Maxwell's *'Til the Cops Come Knockin'* resonated throughout the room. I could hear Renae moan and see her shiver as I began to suck on her clitoris with the ice on the tip of my tongue. I kissed, licked and sucked on her pussy until her sweet nectar poured into my mouth.

The taste of her juices on my tongue caused my dick to stand tall like a good obedient soldier, ATTENTION. Renae smiled once she saw that my blood had once again invaded my manhood. The anticipation of my penis entering her world made her breathe heavy. With one quick smooth move, I put a raincoat on and with my other hand; I put her left leg on my shoulder and began to suck on her inner thigh. Now protected, I grabbed her round, soft ass and slowly penetrated her sugar walls.

I began making love to her using long rhythmic strokes. With each stroke Renae's moans became louder. With her moans becoming louder, my strokes gradually became faster. I pulled out gently, turned her over and entered her from behind; she threw her head back in pleasure. Holding her voluptuous hips, I plunged deeply into her sweet spot trying to submerge every inch of my being inside of her. Renae screamed my name while begging me not to stop. Not wanting the ecstasy to end, I pulled out again and let her mount me like the stallion that I thought I was. Renae straddled me and teasingly brushed her breast across my lips. Slowly lowering herself onto my penis, she moved up and down my shaft like it was a fireman's pole. I bit my lip and my toes began to curl as I controlled my urge to explode. The sensual sounds of her groans began to crescendo and her breathing became more labored. Her moans turned into a guttural sound of "Yes! Yes! Yes!" Her vaginal walls pulsated with delight and I couldn't contain myself any longer. We both climaxed together before she collapsed beside me. Her body became relaxed and I could feel the moistness on her face as she struggled to bring her breathing under control. She turned her face toward me, looked into the eyes of the woman that I was destined to spend the rest of my life with and said, "Damn baby, you ain't just a Ritz girl, you're a gourmet cracker!"

LONNIE SPRY was born in Miami, Florida. He grew up in Forestville, Maryland and graduated from Suitland High School in 1998. As a child, Lonnie developed an early interest in writing poetry from reading the *Songs of Solomon* in the Bible. In high school, Lonnie had a heightened interest in reading Shakespeare in English classes where he continued to hone his writing skills. After much success in writing poems for friends and family, Lonnie was encouraged to write a book of poetry. After many humorous and amusing poems and stories, his friends encouraged him to write a book. While unemployed, he took their advice and his debut novel, *How Do I Go On?* was created.

The Mile High Club

By the time Keema Blackmon arrived, the press conference and luncheon for Jarrett Steele was in full swing. The ballroom at the Fountainbleu Hotel was crowded with members of the press, record industry personnel, and an assortment of artsy types. She even spotted a few groupies who were lucky enough to get in because they knew the right people. Scanning the room, Keema noticed ornate crystal chandeliers and candelabras. The tables were adorned with the finest royal blue linens and fresh-cut black calla lilies were placed strategically in key spots around the space. Her feet were treated to the kind of decadence they hadn't felt in a long time when they were nearly buried in the soft, plush carpeting that had to be at least four inches thick. The publicist for the event seated her at a table right near the podium, then smiled and walked away. Not wanting to miss one word, she took out her Reporter's Notebook and tape recorder to prepare for the event.

Keema reveled in the sound of Jarrett Steele's music permeating the room—its melody filling her ears. Good melodic soul music that was a throwback to the 70's Sound of Philadelphia when real music was in its heyday.

It wasn't long before the table filled up, and the guests seated there introduced themselves, making small talk until the

69

festivities began. There was only one seat left, but it didn't stay empty for long.

Every one of Keema's erogenous zones went on alert—straight into overdrive—as she looked up into the hazel eyes of the finest man she had ever seen. The brother was a good six-foot-five, if he were an inch. He had the most beautiful natural curly hair, a powerfully tight muscular physique, a small gold hoop earring in his left ear, and the kind of honey brown skin that made Keema want to sop him up with a biscuit. To say that he was gorgeous was an understatement.

"Good afternoon," his deep bass voice boomed, resonating in the pit of her loins. Shafts of electricity coursed through Keema's veins as her sienna brown eyes instinctively traveled down to his private area. "Anyone sitting here?"

If that seat were taken, I'd gladly give it away to you. Fuck proper etiquette, she thought, noting the thick, welcome bulge in his crotch, wondering what it would feel like inside of her. "Yes, *you* are."

The smile in his eyes contained a sensuous flame, causing Keema to dream of being crushed in his embrace. A delightful shiver of want ran through every bone in her sex-starved body.

"Thanks," the sexy stranger intoned, his infectious grin pointing up a spark of eroticism. His eyes were compelling, magnetic, filled with a Machiavellian wickedness. "But I'll only be sitting here during the luncheon. Once the press conference begins, I'll be in the Photographer's Pit taking photos." He stood so close to Keema that she felt the heat radiating from his body. It wasn't long before she was thinking under his clothes, wondering what else he could work as well as his camera. She thought about how it would be nice if he could work her body—snapping, fingering, and making magic with any body part he chose—just as he did with photos.

"I'm sure that I'll enjoy every moment you're here; so please, sit," Keema said in invitation to him, ignoring the others at the table. In that moment, she became aware of the blood rushing through her body like an awakened river. She knew that she was flirting, but there was no shame in her game. A man looking *that* good certainly had to be used to it, Keema told herself.

It was then that she noticed his eyes raking boldly over her ample frame, moving from her shoulders to her neck to her full breasts that tingled under his scrutiny. "My mama taught me better than to forget my manners," he quipped. "My name's Erick Toussaint, and what is your name, cher?" Erick took Keema's hand into his and kissed it ever so lightly, appreciating the neat manicure the butterscotch beauty's hand sported.

Explosive currents raced through her and rendered her senseless. "My—name, name is . . . is Keema Blackmon," she stuttered.

"I'm pleased to meet you. That's a beautiful name for a beautiful lady. Who are you covering this for, Keema?" He gently released her hand.

That was it. Keema was toast, and she knew it. Her whole body tingled as he said her name. *Damn, I'm here to get the 411 on Jarrett Steele and his new CD, and this man, who's beyond fine, comes in here and turns my world upside down. You can definitely be my undoing, my brother*, she thought, fanning herself with one of the pages from the press kit that was placed before her. *And, I call myself a professional? Get it together, girlfriend. You're bigger than the prospect of getting what looks like a piece of good dick!*

Finally, Keema replied. "I'm the owner of the Blackmon Communiqué, a new entertainment wire service that feeds entertainment news to media outlets around the world."

By the time the press conference was over, not only did she have everything she needed on Jarrett Steele, but she also learned that Erick had a live-in girlfriend named Yolie. Keema's head told her to tell him to step off and keep it moving, but her loins were ablaze. So she said fuck it, don't worry about it, because she wasn't in the market for a husband—just a decent lay that would make her pussy sing a new song. So when Erick gave her his digits, Keema gave him her real number—not the usual nigga number she'd reserved for the chickenheads and losers she met in clubs. She convinced herself that she didn't care about Yolie because at least Erick was up front about his relationship and didn't try to keep her on the low. She could live with that. After all, Keema was busy trying to get her wire service off the ground and didn't have time for some needy man with issues who wanted to cling to her like a two-year-old to its mother. Still, she backed off because she knew that men smelled desperation in women and desperate, she wasn't—just a vibrant and very horny woman with needs!

As she was nearing the door to leave, Keema felt a feather-light touch on her arm nudging her into an unoccupied area where the crowd had thinned considerably. She tried to protest, but her vocal chords locked up, and nothing intelligible came from her mouth. It wasn't a second later that Erick pulled Keema into his arms, smothering her lips with a kiss that was full of passion and need. Exploring every corner, he claimed her mouth with a savage conquest—his tongue mating with hers—dancing together in a silent melody that only they understood. That kiss was a heady invitation and a challenge that demanded answers, which Keema not only *needed* to, but also *wanted* to give!

The tingling effects of being so close to Erick spread though her like wildfire, his touch triggering primitive yearnings in her trembling body. Keema's throbbing core responded to his adamantine masculinity, and her response was shameless, instant, and total. She tightened her arms around him, crushing his sexy body to hers—its firmness fitting perfectly to the contours of her cushiony curves. The woodsy smell of his Quorum cologne wafted past her nostrils, assaulting every sense Keema thought she had. Soon, she felt the need for a panty liner or a sanitary pad—even—because her juices began to flow like a river—so much so that she felt them running down her leg.

"Keema, you're all woman, cher," Erick moaned, sniffing the primal scent exuded from her natural pheromones. He placed her slightly trembling hand on his steely manhood, encouraging Keema to feel it, rub it, and make it hers.

She marveled at its length and massive girth, wondering how she would take something that size. But as wet as his kiss was making her, Keema was sure that when they got busy for real for real, her kitty would receive everything he had to offer, and Erick Toussaint, the Creole brother from Nawlins, would rock her right!

He gave Keema another kiss—this time, sticking his tongue down her throat—a deep, nasty kiss that branded her his. This round, the dam burst sho nuff, and she couldn't keep still. All she could think about was Erick taking her right there and sticking his colossal dick so far inside of her that it would come out through her throat and his fucking her hard and fast until she cried uncle and begged him to stop and do it again!

"C'est si bon; think about that, mon cher, until we meet again—" he whispered, not doing another thing to take Keema out of her misery. With that, he was out the door like a passing tornado that came through, did major damage, and then moved on.

She knew her toy collection she had long ago affectionately dubbed "Keema's Private Stock," would get a good workout that night.

Erick made good use of her phone number, calling, and e-mailing her several times a day for hot phone sex sessions in which they wouldn't disconnect until they came together and screamed each other's names in unbridled ecstasy. Their busy schedules prevented them from seeing each other too often, but that soon ended when Keema received an invitation to cover Jarrett Steele's CD release party at a new exclusive resort called Connections in Savannah, Georgia.

The invitation said that press members would be driven by limo to the airport to board the private jet provided by Blue Light Records and flown to the venue. Keema's needy pussy— the most erogenous of all the zones in her body—couldn't wait to meet up with Erick's pulsating rod because from all of those nights of his teasing Keema and making her cum with just his words, instinctively, she knew that the brotha could lay some pipe, and Keema planned to be in place for the drilling!

As the members of the press made their way aboard the plane, Steele's publicist was already working his new CD, *Look Into My Heart*, which played in the background. Keema didn't care about the music or any of the other journalists; she was on the lookout for a certain handsome photographer!

Keema's heart nearly jumped out of her chest, beating in double time when, Erick boarded the aircraft mere minutes before the steward locked and secured the door.

He greeted everyone on his way to her. "Comment ca va, cher?" he purred, kissing Keema on both cheeks. His smile was as intimate as one of his sensuous kisses.

"I'm fine now that you're *here*," she said, licking her bow-shaped lips suggestively in response. "I thought you'd *never* arrive."

"I'll always be where you are, cher; no need to ever worry your pretty head about that." He rubbed his crotch and stared

74

into her sparkling sienna brown eyes, his need evident. Keema peeped at the bulge she grew to expect and love.

After the stewards' safety demonstration and preliminary food and beverage service, the flight got underway. It was a smooth ride on that clear day; very little turbulence was felt. The rest of the journalists spoke among themselves, but Erick and Keema had some *other* matters on their minds.

"Come," he lamented, leading her by the hand, a devilish look in his eyes.

Keema did as he asked. An invitation *that* rife with mystery couldn't be ignored. She would've been remiss if she had. The horny beauty was intrigued, to say the least.

Erick led her into the bathroom—which was larger and more accommodating than the ones on commercial flights, and he locked the door behind them.

"You're all mine now, cher, so drop it like it's hot!" he commanded, already removing her miniskirt and satin thong. He wished that they were all alone, so he could tear off her undies. They were getting in his way and impeding progress.

Keema followed Erick's lead and undressed him, removing his pants and silk boxers. Curiosity almost killed her, and she longed to feel his rocked up, elongated jimmy. So she took it in her hands and touched it, familiarizing herself with its shape, smoothness, and every nuance of that part of his anatomy. And just as Keema had surmised from their petting session, Erick was all man.

"Oh baby, you're so big! I can't take all of this cock!"

"Don't worry, cher; you can and you will, and you will enjoy every pleasurable inch," he moaned, obviously confident of his sexual prowess.

At that moment, Keema had to have a taste of his powerful rod. Relaxing her throat muscles, she took him slowly into her mouth, savoring each delicious inch as she sucked him into a state of hysteria. Up and down, round and round, underneath his shaft, and on top. Keema gave equal time to his nuts and to that special spot between the balls and the ass that drives men wild.

"C'est si bon, mon amour," he screamed, ramming his meaty fingers in Keema's boiling cavern. "That's *so* damned good!"

She sucked him until she milked him dry, licking up every drop of his creamy love juice, and asking for more.

Keema wondered if he had a problem with going down into the bush because she sure wanted some head. No problem, there, because Erick proceeded to eat her pulsating pussy like it was an ice cream cone—licking, sucking, fingering, and lapping up every bit of her cum as it squirted into his face.

Keema's world spun totally out of control, and the rumbling of the plane became muted as if she were underwater. Her whole body tingled down to the tips of her toes. "Erick, I'm cumming, baby! I'm cum–"

Her hips gyrated in double time, and she must've cum for a straight fifteen minutes—her love juice squirting and running everywhere. To her way of thinking, the brotha sure knew how to eat some pussy and had turned the act into an art form. Before Keema could come back to her senses, Erick sat her up on the toilet bowl and filled her with so much dick; all she could do was scream out in pleasure and pain. But the pain was sweet, so she bit her lip and endured it.

"Erick, what are you doing to me?" she cried out, locking her legs around his strong, muscular body. "This is some good dick!" Keema surrendered completely to his style of masterful fucking.

"And it's going to get even better, cher. Hang on for the ride, darling!"

Erick rode Keema like a racehorse in the Kentucky Derby—hard, fast, like there was a pussy he had to win. And she enjoyed every sensational long stroke.

She undulated her hips under him, keeping in perfect time to the rhythm he had set. Keema spread her legs even wider, putting her feet against the walls to allow him full access to her aching, hungry cunt.

"That's right, cher, take it," he grunted. "Take *all* of this wood!"

Keema took every inch, every stroke Erick had to give, and she gave it back to him as well as she had gotten, working her muscles—tightening them around his furiously pumping shaft that seemed to have grown even larger.

She felt him hit her G-spot and no longer could she hold back the dam that was building inside of her. "Erick . . . baby . . . . fuck me good," Keema screamed, forgetting that other people were on the plane. Lost in the moment, she cared less and reveled in the feeling of her warm cum coating his dick—the residue running down her legs.

Erick cried out in animalistic release, his cum flowing into Keema like the warmest clover honey.

He came with Keema, then turned her over and gave it to her doggy style until they came so much that they both were worn out and beaten down. They washed themselves up and redressed, then rejoined the rest of the journalists as if nothing happened.

Keema left the bathroom first, then Erick. Both of them had the biggest Kool-Aid grin on their faces, the telltale look of satisfied lovers. They hoped no one knew their secret, but they didn't care if they did. They had gotten their fuck on, and that was good enough for them!

When Keema got back home from the press junket, Erick called and invited her out to a cute little seafood bistro by the river. "Je t'aime, cher," he whispered—gently kissing her hand. "I want to tell you the whole story about Yolie."

"You don't owe me any explanation, Erick," she crooned, cupping and caressing his face. "Did I ever ask you to give me one?"

"No, you didn't, sweetie, but I love you and want to share everything in my life with you—even *this*. Please allow me to do that."

"Go ahead." She stood there, stark-still, as if fastened to the wall behind her. She began to listen with great trepidation because she didn't want to lose him to his live-in lover. She was sprung and wanted him all to herself—although she'd never tell him that.

"A couple of years ago, I went through a major financial crisis," he recounted, his brow furrowing. The tiny lines in his forehead became more pronounced. Then, Erick continued. "A paparazzi competitor stole important slides from my studio, then he set it afire. I lost everything, and the insurance company was real slow in its investigation. See, they had to make sure that I didn't burn it down myself to get the claim money. I was uptight, broke, and penniless, and I had just purchased a home over in the Garden District. I was about to lose it to foreclosure. Desperate, I called Yolie, the only person I knew whom I could depend on. She came up from New York and moved in, and we became co-owners of the home."

"It was nice of her to give up her life and move down here to help you," Keema sighed, not wanting to hear anymore lies from Erick's sexy lips. "You two must be very close."

Erick seemed pensive; his admission was dredged between a place beyond logic and reason. "We are; she's my *half-sister*."

"Your half-sister?" The heavy lashes that shadowed Keema's cheeks flew up. She took in a quick intake of breath, the shock of discovery hitting her full force. Keema was both shocked and pleased at his revelation. "Why did you tell me she was your girlfriend?"

"I do that as a defense mechanism when I first meet women," Erick explained, taking Keema's hand into his. "I meet a lot of crazies, so I do that to put some distance between us—to protect my heart if things don't work out. I'm sorry for telling a lie. Forgive me, cher?"

Keema forgave Erick and kissed him like a madwoman right in the middle of the restaurant—not giving two shits who saw them. She loved that man, and she was pulling out all the stops to make him hers.

∾ ∾ ∾ ∾ ∾

One Year Later

Since last year, Yolie invited Keema for dinner where she showed her a birth certificate proving that she and Erick had the same father. Their mutual affection for Erick made them become fast friends. As for Keema's relationship with Erick, they are quite the item. They spend every available moment they're together fucking each other's brains out in every conceivable position in the most unorthodox places. He continues to keep Keema's juices flowing when he talks dirty to her in French. She doesn't know what the future holds for her and Erick, but she knows one thing: she is madly in love with Erick and he with her. Keema will be open to whatever he suggests—with Yolie's blessings!

★ ★ ★ ★ ★

NATHASHA BROOKS-HARRIS lives and works in New York City where she successfully juggles a government career with the demands of being a romance author. Her latest book, *Can I Get An Amen Again*, (an anthology with co-authors Kim Louise, Janice Sims, and Natalie Dunbar), is the follow-up to the Emma Award-nominated *Can I Get An Amen*. Her debut romance novel, *Panache*, was released to her worldwide fans in 2001, earning her the prestigious Emma Award for Best New Author. She is the former Editor-in-Chief of *Black Romance*, *Bronze Thrills*, and *True Confessions* magazines. In addition, she freelances as a Contributing Editor at *Today's Black Woman* magazine, where she writes the popular monthly departments "Career and Money News," "Career Savvy" and a women's general information column called "FYI." Brooks-Harris has also been a book reviewer for *QBR* magazine, SORMag, Romance In Color, and The Romer Review websites. She's a contributor for the *Gumbo For The Soul* website, where she writes about breaking into writing and getting successfully published. She is the co-founder of the romance writing website devoted to women romance authors of color, The Wonderful Women of Romance—a part of The Belles & Beaux of Romance, where she was formerly a reviewer. Brooks-Harris is proud to have an essay about literacy in the recently-released *Gumbo For the Soul* anthology—endorsed by the well-respected author and TV personality, Tavis Smiley. When she's not writing, she teaches the craft of writing at the prestigious Frederick Douglas Center For Creative Arts. In her spare time, Brooks-Harris is a cloth dollmaker and quilter—whose work has appeared in several museum exhibitions and fiber art magazines. She may be reached at writernbh@yahoo.com.

keySTROKES

Debra tossed her keys on her end table as she walked in from work. Her eyes darted around the empty living room, immediately going to the etched glass clock that hung above her fireplace.

6:35 P.M.

Her heart jumped in her chest, for she knew *he* would be waiting for her. But, she wasn't ready. She hadn't showered yet, and her stomach was growling at her, begging to be fed.

Charles, her husband, was out of town at a conference, working as usual. Though she needed no reminder of their present situation, she knew that was his way of avoiding being at home, but she didn't care anymore. It was like fighting a losing battle, over and over again. When he left the message, telling her he would be home tonight, her pulse remained steady even though she wanted to scream. Debra liked when he was gone, doing whatever it was he did at those things during those moments of solitude. She had become very skillful at finding ways to entertain herself when he was away.

As she stood in the kitchen, dicing tomatoes for her salad, her face warmed with every thought of *him*. Smiling when she thought of the last time they were together. *He* had a way of making her legs quiver and her pussy throb to the rhythm of his conversation. Licking her lips at the thought of taking him in her mouth, Debra envisioned herself sucking him drier than a James Bond martini. After a quiver, she chuckled. There was no way she could do that without rehearsal and be good at it, she thought, for she was more out of practice than Terrell Owens before a Monday night game.

Her and Charles' sex life was non-existent. His touch was empty and her heart was hardened. Sex was more like a job than an act of sheer pleasure between two people who loved each other.

Finding a place at her kitchen table, the intimate setting for one was illuminated by the track lighting that hung above the bay window. She reached up and freed her hair from the confines of her ponytail.

She checked the clock on the stove.

8:45 P.M.

Smirking slightly, she continued to eat her dinner made for one of salad and grilled chicken. *I wonder if he's waiting for me,* she thought.

While loading the sterling silver appliance with what she had, she decided not to run it until the end of the week. It was getting late.

He would be waiting.

Totally relaxed, Debra made her way to the bathroom, turning the huge glass knobs causing the shower to rumble to life. Water poured from the spout and she ran her hand through it, making sure to get the temperature just right. Removing her uniform, she stared at her birthday suit in the mirror. She wasn't happy with what she saw. A fit size fourteen, kissing the nose of a size sixteen, small waist and average sized breast. In the shower, she let the water run over her body, further relaxing her. Dipping her head under the soothing waterfall, she allowed the warmth to force the stress from her. Her breathing quickened for a second at the thought of *him.*

He told her he would be waiting for her tonight. That was her fuel to get her through the day. The thought of him anticipating, then, arousing her, the exquisite erotic images that came to mind whenever she thought of him caused her thick frame to tremble.

After drying off, she didn't bother to put on clothes. A silk red robe would be all she needed. No bra, no panties. Debra sat on the edge of the bed and began rubbing lavender scented baby oil into her still damp skin.

Her pussy purred, begging for attention as she rubbed the oil into her thighs. Squeezing a little harder than necessary and allowing her thumb to brush against her moist mound, a soft moan rose in her throat. Acknowledging her touch, but still embarrassed by it nonetheless, she felt the butterflies take flight in her stomach.

The blood rushed to her pelvic area, enlivening it, encouraging her to do what she considered unthinkable. Her self-massage continued as she moved to her arms. Rubbing the warm oil into her shoulders, she dropped her hand a little. Sweeping her hand across her now exposed breast, she allowed her fingers to brush against her rock hard nipples. They stood at attention, passionately pleading for her touch. Licking her lips as she began rubbing her calf. Hadn't she already done them? Debra felt her face become warm with embarrassment from what she was doing. That soon didn't matter as she found her hand traveling back up her shapely leg again until it rested on her inner thigh. She spread her fingers, palming the warm flesh, squeezing it as she moved her hand closer to her now wet crotch. She tried to block out what she was doing, pretend that every time her thumb tickled, teased and tweaked her throbbing clit, that it was an accident. But her quickening breath and her pouted nipples would tell a different story.

She glanced at the clock.

10:00 P.M.

The smile returned to her face as she returned to the living room. Taking a seat at the computer desk nestled in the far corner of the dark space, the red light from the LCD monitor was the only glow the room needed.

She logged into her Instant Messenger. All of her smiley faces were gray. Their animated faces mimicking a deep slumber, a wave of sadness captured her.

He wasn't online.

Her heart sank as she logged out and logged back in, hoping that somehow the small box had made a mistake that his smiley would somehow magically come to life. She was still online alone. Excitement warring with disappointment, she even sent him a message, asking if he was invisible. Sometimes he did that to avoid being seen online by anyone.

No reply.

She tightened the belt on her silk robe, and began to aimlessly search the Internet.

Amazon.com. She ordered a couple of books.

Sears.com. She priced a new, high-definition television.

Hotmail.com. No new emails, just junk.

Promises of a bigger penis if she sent $29.95 for a bottle of pills.

Coupons from Bath and Body Works offering deep discounts with huge orders.

Delete.

Delete.

Delete.

11:00 P.M.

She yawned, reached up and got ready to pull her still damp hair back into a ponytail.

That's when she heard it. That tiny knock on the door of her computer screen.

The sound that announced *he* was here, causing her vaginal walls to contract.

She smiled as the small chat box expanded and illuminated her screen.

Black Prince: *What are you doing online this late?*

Cinderella24: *waiting for you*

Black Prince: *Yeah, right...I've been here. I've just been busy watching TV.*

Black Prince: *I saw when you asked if I were invisible. I didn't answer because I was watching TV.*

No he didn't! Debra thought.

Cinderella24: *that's mean!!*

Black Prince: *I know but I'm on my Blackberry. I don't like typing on it too much. It's not like my computer.*

Cinderella24: *I see...*

Black Prince: *Are you still my friend?*

Cinderella24: *Of course...*

Black Prince: *Did you think about me today?*

Cinderella24: *yes I did...a little more than I should have, I might add.*

Black Prince: *Hello...*

Cinderella24: *i'm here, lol*

Feeling flushed once more, Debra was sure her caramel-colored skin was highlighted with the red undertones of her blush. Her eyes cut to the front door. Knowing that Charles could be coming through it soon added to the excitement of what she was doing, making her blood race through her veins.

Black Prince: *Just say it... don't be shy...*

Cinderella24: *lol*

Cinderella24: *i have been over the top with my flirting lately*

Black Prince: *Are you apologizing? What were (or is) your intentions behind it?*

Black Prince: *Okay...to make it simple...Why?*

Cinderella24: *why was I flirting?*

Black Prince: *Yes*

Cinderella24: *it was intentional, to answer your question*

Cinderella24: *not sure why.....*

Black Prince: *I don't believe that...*

Cinderella24: *why?*

Black Prince: *I don't believe people intentionally do things without knowing why.*

Black Prince: *It doesn't make sense...*

Cinderella24: *don't go all analytical on me....*

Black Prince: *Not being analytical...*

Pressing her thighs together in a futile effort to quell her excitement, she found that her pussy throbbed intensified. Wishing that he could come through the screen and feel the brewing flood between her legs, she reached up and ran her fingers across her computer screen.

Cinderella24: *okay... maybe i just find myself attracted to you.....*

Black Prince: *What?*

Black Prince: *Hello?*

Cinderella24: *i am here...*

Cinderella24: *it's just odd for me that's all*

Cinderella24: *does that bother you?*

Black Prince: *No...it sounds like it bothers you...*

Cinderella24: *no it doesn't bother me... just weird... we're miles away... but it's like I crave you...*

Black Prince: *I don't believe you...*

Cinderella24: *i swear...*

Black Prince: *Prove it...*

Cinderella24: *what do you mean...?*

Black Prince: *you know what I mean...cum for me*

As if hypnotized, instinctively she reached down, pulled the satiny material of the belt that held together her robe. She knew what he wanted; because she wanted the same thing.

Cinderella24: *I could get in a LOT of trouble with you.*

Black Prince: *True...but that's what you want isn't it?*

Her nipples hardened, he knew her better than she wanted him to know. They had shared many intimate nights comforting each other via cyber space. Him bringing her to orgasms so sticky she had to wipe down her keyboard after she was done. The only thing she knew of him was his screen name and that his words somehow had power over her.

Black Prince: *Hello???*

Cinderella24: *i'm here!*

Black Prince: *you like the way I make your pussy come to life... don't you?*

Cinderella24: *yes...*

Her fingers were drawing circles around her luscious mounds by now. Coaxing them to attention with every stroke, the friction from the silky material of her robe, mixed with the sensation her fingers were giving her, was sending Debra over the top. Running her tongue across her lips, wetting them while wishing he were there to fill her empty orifice with all he had to offer, she moaned.

Black Prince: *Everyday I know that you're thinking about me...*

Black Prince: *Fantasizing about what you want me to do to you...*

Cinderella24: *don't do that.....*

Black Prince: *you want me to stop?*

She didn't want him to stop and he knew that. He was playing mind games, the kind she enjoyed. The kind she couldn't dare tell anyone about.

Cinderella24: *no... please don't*

Black Prince: *I'm letting my desires run wild. That's not very good. I may want to take advantage of the situation.*

Cinderella24: *talk to me...*

Her mind and body, aroused and ablaze all at once, had her craving this man in every way; and there was no explanation for it. A man she had never seen, never touched, but was the constant star of her most erotic dreams. He was a faceless stranger, touching her, testing, teasing and tasting her senses, sexing her like crazy. Making her shudder and shake by day, he had her spellbound, making her pussy quiver and quake as they conversed, and causing her to have orgasms in her sleep that would wake her at odd hours of the night, inducing a smile from her before peacefully drifting off to sleep again.

Black Prince: *r u doing what I told you...*

Her mouth was thick with saliva. She swallowed hard. Her breathing was quickening.

Cinderella24: *Yes.*

Black Prince: *I don't believe you... do it...*

Cinderella24: *okay...*

She reached down, her hands finding the top of her exposed thigh. Almost as if on autopilot, her legs separated in the chair. As if he could see her, he gave her commands. And, she followed them.

Black Prince: *touch it... pretend it's me...*

Obeying, her fingers made their way to her soaking wet cavern. She scooted down in the chair, resting her foot on the small bookshelf next to the desk, and spreading her legs wider. She wished at that moment she had a webcam, so he could see how wet she was.

Black Prince: *how does it feel, tell me...*

She positioned herself so she could type with her free hand while she continued to run her fingers along her labia, getting lost in the warmth and the wetness.

Her fingers were sloppy wet as her juices seeped from her body, pooling in the leather chair beneath her. She looked down at her body; saw her skin beginning to glow with perspiration.

Black Prince: *talk to me...tell me...is your pussy wet?*

Cinderella24: *yes...*

Cinderella24: *real wet...feels so damn good...*

Black Prince: *wht do you plan on doing abt it?*

Black Prince: *This damn phone...*

Smiling at his typos, Debra imagined that he had his dick in his hand, manipulating and masturbating his manhood to masculinity.

Cinderella24: *r u touching urself?*

It was damn hard to type with one hand, but she was too far gone to stop now. She needed this. She needed him.

Black Prince: *I have my dick in my hand now...wish you were here...r u fingering yourself?*

Cinderella24: *yes...*

Black Prince: *I want to taste you...tell me what you taste like...*

She struggled to fight against the storm brewing inside of her. She slid one finger into her warmth. Moving it in and out with the skill that she imagined he would have if he were there. Her breasts swelled even larger with every breath she sucked in and blew out. She pulled her finger out, spying the juices glistening from it. Without hesitation, she sucked the member into her mouth, running circles around it with her tongue. She imagined it was him buried in the warmth of her mouth. She hungrily lapped up her juices, growing more and more intoxicated from the taste of her honey pot. Scooping some more of her nectar, she happily gobbled it up from her sticky fingers.

Cinderella24: *umm... sweet*

Black Prince: *i bet u r...damn, my mouth is watering...*

Cinderella24: *don't make me cum alone...*

Black Prince: *you're not alone baby...my dick is harder than Chinese math...*

She imagined him, sitting in front of his computer, legs splayed, dick in hand.

One finger.

Pulling on it. Up, then down. Beads of sweat forming on his forehead as he swelled and twitched in his hand. Using his finger to spread the pre-cum along his shaft.

Two fingers.

Curling his hand around his dark manhood that was getting harder with each stroke. She imagined his face twisted with a desire. Reaching up, she cupped her breast, gently but forcibly tugging at her erect nipple. She buried her fingers deep inside her moist folds as her mouth fell open with a loud gasp.

Three fingers.

Black Prince: *I want you to cum for me baby....make yourself cum.*

She closed her eyes, leaned back in the chair and pictured them in an empty room; him having her pinned against the wall while he worked her pussy from behind. Slamming into her, causing her whole body to shake, he made her call out in a pleasurable pain that felt so, so good. Filling her with every inch of his hot tool, his strokes in fantasy were fervent, frantic and furious. Her legs shook, causing the pictures atop the book case to wobble then fall.

Black Prince: *damn baby, how many fingers are in your pussy right now...*

Cinderella24: *3*

That was all she could manage to type. Her thoughts were not her own. Her body was consumed with fire. That fire threatened to burn down her house around her. The sloppy wet sounds coming from her pussy were driving her over the edge. She could feel her orgasm building. Sweat ran down her body, mixing with the juices from her wet cavern.

Cinderella24: *bout 2 cum...*

Black Prince: *me too baby...cum for me...*

Her orgasm rode her body like a freight train, shaking her from head to toe.

She let out a loud gasp as her pussy contracted around the fingers she had buried deep within. She reached up, pinched her nipple, squeezing it so hard that it sent shock waves to her pelvis. A flood of sweet, hot liquid spilled from her, running out onto the chair and oozing between her fingers. She fought to catch her breath, reaching up wiping the sweat from her forehead.

A noise that sounded like a car door brought her back to her reality. She looked towards the small clock in the corner of the computer screen.

12:15 A.M.

It was too early for Charles to be home. He said he would be here after one. Panicked, Debra jumped up from her seat, and rushed to the window in her bedroom. She heaved a sigh of relief to see the space next to her car still empty. On the way back to the living room she caught a glimpse of herself in the mirror and smiled. Her hair was disheveled and tangled, skin moist with sweat. Who would've thought that *he* would be one of her hottest lovers?

Black Prince: *u ok?*

Cinderella24: *yes...*

Black Prince: *I'm going to bed now...I'll talk with you tomorrow.*

Cinderella24: *okay*

Cinderella24: *sweet dreams*

Black Prince: *I think they'll be a little too sweet...*

Cinderella24: *good night...*

Black Prince: *good night my love...*

While she's cleaning up she hears the phone ringing. The answer machine comes to life and her voice fills the empty room.

"Hello, you have reached the residence of Pastor and Mrs. Charles Smith..."

★ ★ ★ ★ ★

D.L.SPARKS is a freelance writer and author of *Never Say Never* and *All That Glitters*. In February 2007, D.L. established Hightower Editorial Services. Currently, she reside outside of Atlanta with her husband and two kids.

Gettin' Served

The delicate fragrance floated seductively through the air and left a desirable trail teasing and taunting Peter, as he searched intensively throughout the crowded restaurant in hopes of finding its origin. Trying not to allow the obvious to distract him, he continued eating his rock lobster, while shooting the breeze with his best friend, Chris.

Warm as the sun, dipped in black, Peter was a tall glass of water, standing at a muscular six-foot-two, adorning a perfectly sculpted goatee, laced around full, yet sensual lips. He commanded attention, wherever he went, and tonight was no different.

Friday night dinners were the norm for Chris and Peter for many years now. After attending both grammar and high school together, and then off to the same college, it was a ritual they maintained. Peter was happy to be hanging out with his main man, but was heavily distracted by this woman, a true vision of beauty, he thought, a body to add to the mysterious fragrance.

"Can I get you guys anything else," the waitress asked, all the while staring deeply into Peter's eyes. Finally, he was able to locate the arousing smell that had been under his nose all along.

Glancing up at the tall African American woman, dressed in a skimpy black top, with blue skinny jeans that held on to a scrumptious and full bottom, Peter instantly became turned on, and the swelling between his thighs was at an all time high. Thank God no one could see the distraction that lie behind his zipper, he thought. Gray, almond shaped eyes, peered at Peter while he thought about how to answer the waitress' question, without getting her to leave him again so quickly.

Chris interrupted Peter, momentarily pulling him from a trance, and responded to her. "We may have coffee. Oh, can we see a dessert menu?"

"Sure," the waitress responded, before walking away to get the coffee and menus.

"Man, did you see the booty on Mami?" Peter asked, while still following the waitress' every move as she walked away.

"Did I? Shit, I couldn't help it. But man, damn, you so obvious," Chris said, laughing at his boy.

"Yo, man, all I need is five minutes with her. Just five minutes and I'd be a happy man," Peter confessed, after tossing a rolled up napkin at Chris.

"Man, yeah, me too. I think I'll ask for her number."

"Really?"

"I mean, if that's okay with you, Pete."

"Yeah, man, it's cool. Give it a try."

"Thanks, man, I will." Chris turned around to see if the waitress was nearby.

As she approached, with two coffees in hand, she sat them down in front of Peter, then in front of Chris, leaning in so that each of the two strangers could get an eye-popping view of her double-D, honey-coated cleavage. And as she suspected, both Chris and Peter stared, in amazement, at the beauty only a woman of color could possess. Leaning up slowly, she looked into Peter's eyes first, then into Chris', while handing them each a dessert menu.

94

"I'll give you a few minutes to decide on what you want for dessert," she said as a sly smile parted her luscious pink lips, coated in Mac lip glass.

With the boldness of a cobra, Chris gently tugged at her arm. "Are you on the menu, sweetie?"

With a coy smile, coupled with sexy confidence, once again she leaned in close, in the center of the table, to give a birds-eye view of seduction in its most deep and pure form. "Well, that depends..."

Looking at both her and Peter, Chris responded, "Depends on what?"

"...if the two of you will be having dessert."

With a smile that defines the word "cheese," Peter leaned in and said, "So you'll be the dessert, if the two of us want to eat it?"

"Exactly," she challenged and walked away.

Peter felt his nature rise, once more, as he captured the bounce to her stride from behind.

"Yo, is she serious?" Chris asked.

"I'm not sure. I think she's playing, man. But can you imagine?"

"Yeah, Pete, she's nice and thick, in all the right places too. I could have a ball with her."

Returning to take the dessert order, "By the way, I'm Lana," she made known, as a sensually arousing smile emphasized her full lips.

"Nice to meet you, Lana," Chris said as he kissed the back of her hand.

Taking her other hand, Peter kissed it. "So nice to meet you, I'm Pete and my boy is Chris."

"Have the two of you decided?"

"On you, or dessert, pretty lady?"

"Both, Chris."

"Well, Lana, I guess we would want to skip dessert here, and get right to eating you."

"Is that right?"

"It could never be wrong, Lana. All you have to do is say yes."

"Yes."

"Perfect. Do you have a ride?"

"Yes, I do Chris. Where should I meet the two of you?"

Peter jumped in. "I'll reserve the penthouse at the W Hotel. It's just a few blocks away. Just go to Peter LaCrosse's suite."

"Will do. I'll be there in about an hour."

Peter and Chris hopped into Peter's new ride, a 2007 Dodge Aspen, fully-loaded, in silver metallic. It had just enough room in its interior for two NBA players. Both Chris and Peter played for the local team. Big boys, with big appetites, big money, and big sexual desires. Both stood at an attractive and attentive six-foot-two, with golden brown skin and professional athlete dental work, which made their smiles light up the night. Wearing size fifteen and sixteen shoes, respectively, Peter and Chris packed more than just heavy wallets. They were packing heat between their thighs, and could deliver deep blows to any vagina that had enough nerve to open wide.

Glancing over to Peter, who was driving at the time, Chris expressed his disbelief in what was about to go down. "Yo, Pete, man, she look good as hell, man."

"She damn sure do. Remind me of Jennifer Hudson a little bit."

"Yeah? I can't see that, but I can see those big titties and that big, juicy booty right now. She kinda look like Tocarra to me. I'm gonna hit that in the worst way."

"Chris, I think we'll take turns with her. Have some respect. She probably would feel better that way."

"Alright, Pete, I'm down with that."

Arriving at the W Hotel, in the heart of New York City, the valet took the keys from Peter, and they proceed to rent a suite, in preparation for the serious orgasmic experience that was about to take place.

The palatial suite was built for a king. Plush ivory carpets, a fully-stocked bar, a massive king-sized bed, a huge living area with a fifty-inch flat screen and sound system, made the suite feel more like a luxury home, rather than a hotel. Peter prepared Chevis Regal on ice, with a splash of orange juice for him and Chris, walked over to Chris, and handed him the drink. He glanced at the clock that read eleven, and at the same time, the doorbell to the suite rang. Both Peter and Chris almost knocked each other down, fighting to get to the door first. Chris beat Peter to the punch, and opened the door for Lana. He took her by the hand, and led her into the suite, and as she walked further into the suite, Chris glared at her bountiful backside and thick thighs.

"Thanks for having me, Peter and Chris. I'm looking forward to having a good time," Lana said, while removing her lightweight, black Baby Phat jacket.

"Would you like a drink, Lana?" Peter asked while standing at the bar.

"Sure, I'll have whatever you're having."

"So, are you ready to feed us dessert, Lana?" Chris asked, approaching her.

"Whenever you boys are ready to double-dip, I'm ready. I got something sweet for you."

"Is that right?" Peter asked, handing Lana her drink.

She took a sip. Lana was sitting on the sofa in the living area, sandwiched between Chris and Peter. "You make a good drink, Peter."

"Why, thank you, Lana. You make for good eye-candy."

"Thank you, Peter, and I taste good too."

"Is that right?" Peter asked. "Can I get a taste?"

"Anytime," Lana responded, kicking off her shoes and running her toes through the plush carpet.

"Nice feet," Chris said to her, dropping to his knees in front of her.

"Nice lips too," Peter told her as he inched in toward her face. He slipped his tongue between her lips, giving her a soft French kiss. "And they taste good, too," Peter told Chris.

As Peter kissed Lana more, he rubbed her breasts with his strong, masculine hands, making her nipples hard as a rock. Chris kissed her pretty little feet, and sucked her cherry red painted toes. The sensation both men gave her made Lana anxious with desire. She moaned, loud heavy moans as Peter sucked on her nipples and cupped her breasts into his hands. The lust got the best of her. Lana reached her petite hand down to her crotch, where the heat rose from the dead, and began to play with herself through her jeans.

Chris stopped her and removed her hand. "I'll take care of that for you, baby."

Peter went back and forth, from Lana's neck to her breasts, to her lips with his tongue, and Chris unbuttoned her pants, slid them down her legs, over her feet, and tossed them to the side, exposing an already saturated vagina that drenched the black-laced thong she was wearing.

Pulling the thong off, Chris' mouth watered as he thought about the feast he was about to embark on—tasty, sweet pussy hairs first, then a juice-soaked pussy, with a throbbing clitoris that begged for his attention. "Damn, Lana. It's like that? You look good, baby," Chris said, as he began to taste Lana. Eating and sucking on her pussy made Chris' dick hard as steel, and his dick, now in steel-bat status, made its way out of his khakis.

"Mmmm, Chris, eat that pussy and make it come," she said while gyrating on his face.

Meanwhile, Peter removed his jeans, and his thick manhood fell out of his Calvin Klein boxer briefs and the tip landed on her lips, spilling pre-come across her lips. "Mmm, Lana, you gonna suck that dick, right?" Peter asked while rubbing her breasts. Lana's tongue slowly crept out of her mouth, slithering and licking the pre-come, creating a drooling effect, smearing onto her glossy lips that turned Peter on in the worst way.

Chris was still having fun eating her delight and admired the cream that rose to the top from the mastery of his mouth. Placing his fingers into her wonder, Chris literally wondered why he hadn't taken a dip into something so prime and ripe and ready for entry. He looked up and saw how skillfully Lana was sucking Peter's dick, and that made him want to handle business right away. She was more than sexy at the moment. Spreading her legs far, and wide, Chris stroked his manhood, and gave Lana the tip.

"Oooh," she gagged, while her mouth still clutched around the growing mushroom headed cock, sucking Peter into a state of euphoria. Chris, turned on to the tenth power, thrust into Lana, giving her all nine, thick inches deeply, causing an erotic explosion from Lana, as evidenced by the saturation of his dick, wet and wild in ecstasy. He slid out and in over and over, forcing Lana to take it all in, pleasing every wall of her sweetness, left to right, side to side, up and down, hitting all angles, stirring into his self-proclaimed dessert and, as he glanced up again, he saw the visual of Peter's release onto Lana's face, the result of too much heat and passion, more than he could bear. As Peter stroked his dick, Lana welcomed all remnants of his lust into her mouth as she devoured his ejaculation.

"Ah shit, Lana," Peter said as he rubbed the tip across her lips, providing her with a "Got Milk" look to add to his visual and physical pleasure.

Rocking in and out, Chris tried to hold onto the feeling as long as he could, but that dizzying high he anticipated all night took over him—mind, body, and soul—forcing him to pull out. Dick shiny, wet and drenched with Lana's love, he stroked it, allowing the light cream to splatter all over her now delightfully swollen pussy lips. "Damn, girl," Chris expelled.

Peter had gone into the bathroom, and brought back a warm washcloth and cleaned Lana's face, then leaned in, and washed her vagina. Looking up at him, Lana was appreciative, of both the intense sexual pleasure, and the dose of respect in the aftermath. "Thank you, Peter. I really needed that."

"You're welcome, Lana, I needed that too. I hope you enjoyed yourself."

"I damn sure did," Chris responded, after returning from the bathroom, to clean himself off.

"I could use another drink. Does anyone else want one?" Peter asked as he headed to the bar area once more.

"Sure," Both Chris and Lana responded simultaneously.

The infamous sofa, where the ménage claimed its origin, was exactly where all three involved were seated. Sipping on their alcohol, Chris flickered through all channels, with the remote, when Lana interrupted.

"I could go for some more dessert, fellas."

Chris glared at Lana in amazement, and responded, "Word?" Putting his drink on the coffee table, he reached over to Lana, removed her black laced bra, and began to suck on her nipples, a

100

true reversal of roles, taking Peter's place from earlier, during the sexual escapade. He went from her tits to her lips, and tongued her something fierce.

Lana felt her heat rising once more and demanded to be served the way she wanted to be. "Wait, Chris. Let me get some from the back." She kneeled onto the sofa and placed her luscious, round, golden ass in mid air, gyrating and slapping the ass cheeks, while she provided more eye-candy for Chris and Peter.

"Damn, girl, you ready, I see," Peter confessed as he let his pants once again fall to the floor. He stepped out of them, placed his knees on the sofa, mounted himself behind Lana and rubbed his dick across her ass, up and down the ass crack, smacked her cheeks a few times. He placed his thumb into her asshole and slid it in and out a few times, which drove Lana wild. Chris moved in front of her, and placed his tip into her mouth, hoping that he would get the same fabulous head job that his boy received some time ago.

Peter slid into Lana's hot, wet, and sticky vagina from the rear and plunged into her hard and deep, forcing her body to move back and forth in rhythm to Peter. He maintained a clear visual of a shiny, banging set of ass cheeks, and saw his dick, as it stirred in and out, round and round, becoming more and more slick with each blow.

"Aaah, Lana, you got some good ass pussy," Peter confessed, while the friction from Lana's pretty hole, made his head spin in desire.

"Yeah, man, she has some sweet ass," Chris expelled, while trying to hold onto an inevitable ejaculation.

Chris looked down, and the bobbing of Lana's head, along with serious dick sucking she provided, made a volcanic eruption from Chris into Lana's mouth. Lana, who made his orgasm good to the last drop, enjoyed her dessert. And, Peter, now in a state of multiple satisfactions, released more of his desert onto Lana's ass before he bent over her left ass cheek, and licked his own orgasm. "I like this kind of desert. What a way to get served."

CHINA BLUE is a well-known author and poet. Her real identity has not yet been revealed.

Please visit China at www.myspace.com/chinablueonline or email chinablueonline@yahoo.com.

Discovering Love

Trina eyed the gasoline pump as she swiped her credit card. *There goes dinner tonight.* She had to fill up her tank, had to stretch out every penny. Gasoline prices were sky high, and her measly bonus hadn't helped at all. She kept her eye on the pump, watching the numbers soar, her disappointment growing with each click of the meter. When the pump passed $50.00, with no signs of slowing down, she gave up watching the meter and slowly gazed around her. A typical beautiful day in Maryland. Beautiful black folk in their car toys were filling up all around her. One young girl jumped into her two-door Mercedes Benz, top down, shades on. *Wonder what it feels like to have folks with money.*

She turned her head toward the sound of music blasting from a grey sports car. It was one of her favorite songs, a club hopper that she wouldn't dare listen to in front of her uptight husband. James only listened to jazz and slow jams, which was why Trina loved days like today, when he was traveling, the baby was with her mother, and she could ride around in her car, windows down and hip hop music blasting. She could let loose and remember the time before she was the prim and proper wife, when she snuck kisses behind the bleachers or danced a slow grind with her boyfriend in the middle of the dance floor.

Perfect day. Except for the damn gas prices. Pushing her shades back, she focused on the light brown face behind the driver seat of the sports car. *What kinda car is that?* She didn't realize she was staring until the man behind the wheel smiled. Trina jumped, as the nozzle in her hand clicked. *I'm standing out here staring like a fool.* She replaced the nozzle on the pump, careful not to look in the direction of the smiling man, and reached for a paper towel from the dispenser. Quickly climbing into her Ford Explorer, Trina realized she needed to clean her windshield. She quickly climbed out of her truck, and, keeping her eyes lowered, located the windshield mop.

"Mrs. Long?"

Trina turned suddenly to see the light brown man standing behind her. *Damn.* She could feel her heart rate quicken at the thought of standing next to such a beautiful man.

"Mrs. Long, right?"

"Yeah?" Trina smiled, looking directly at him for the first time. *Pull yourself together, girl, he is young enough to be your baby brother.* He seemed familiar. "Don't I know you?"

"You don't remember me? Brian. I used to play football with—"

"Terrance." *Of course. Damn. Who woulda thought you could grow into two hundred pounds of masculine wonderland? Keep your eyes focused on his neck and face, girl, don't look down at his chest. Or his feet.* "Of course I remember you."

They looked at each other for an awkward second, and then he moved in for the friendly hug, which she normally would have offered had he not been so gorgeous. She silently chastised herself for not relaxing and gave him a gentle hug, careful not to fully touch him.

"So how is Terrance? What is he up to?"

"Still playing. Senior year." She threw the wiper mop back into the pail. "What about you?"

"Pro. Six years ago."

"Of course I knew that. Congratulations." *Has it been six years*? "I am losing time, or it's going by too fast. Terrance went to the draft party, right?"

"Yeah man, it was huge. Kinda like a dream. Then, anyway. Real life now."

"I am so proud of you. We watch you, you know. I just haven't seen you in person in so long, or without a helmet, that it took me a moment."

"You watch the games?"

Well, not really. James always watched, she just checked in long enough to see him do something, to cheer on her brother's friend, the little boy who had the cute little crush on her. "Naw, I just watch you." She shrugged and smiled.

"Aw, still no patience for football, huh?"

They both laughed.

"So, is that your car?"

"Yep. Taking the Maserati for a spin."

"So, how is this life? Is it everything you dreamt of? You always talked about being famous, making millions...."

"Yeah, its good. I can't really complain. I like not being famous though. Get to play and live life. A lot of stress, though. And the expectations are bizarre. I can't believe how important the little things are, and how no one seems to care about what matters."

She nodded. She knew all about expectations. Sometimes she felt like she was suffering, drowning under them. They stood there for a moment, staring at each other.

"So, it is Mrs. Long, right? You are actually married, huh?"

Trina nodded slowly. "Yeah, the wedding was the same week as your party. That's why I missed it."

"Yeah, I remember. How is married life treating you?"

She shrugged and smiled. "I can't complain, I guess."

He observed her quietly. She knew she should have given a more enthusiastic answer, but she just couldn't.

"Well," she said, slowly, "I better get going. It was wonderful seeing you. You should keep in touch." The look in his eye changed slightly. She suddenly became flushed. She hadn't meant for it to come out like that, so throaty. She had meant to keep it light, to say that he should keep in touch with Terrance. "I mean, you and Terrance were real close and, you know, we like to see you."

He smiled, but his eyes remained locked on hers. "Yeah, I will…keep in touch with you, Terrance." They stared at each other for another moment. "It was good seeing you, Mrs. Long."

Her married name. He had never called her that before today, she realized. "Trina. Still Trina."

"Trina," he said it much softer. "It was good seeing you, Trina."

"Alright, well you take care of yourself." This time she took the step closer for the friendly departing hug. This time there was no space between the two of them.

He took a couple of steps backward, his eyes still on her. Then he smiled and turned toward his car.

What the hell was that? Trina knocked the sunglasses back onto her face and climbed in her SUV. Her hands were shaking and she felt flushed. How long has it been since someone had looked at her in that way? Had actually looked at her like they wanted to devour her. She couldn't remember.

Stop it. He is a child. If he was the same age as her little brother, he was a full ten years her junior. *He is just flirting to see if he can get away with it. To test how many folks turn groupie now that he is a pro football player. Stop trippin'.*

She started her engine and began to pull out of the gas station. As she waited for traffic to clear for her to turn right, the wide gray sports car pulled up along side her.

"Trina!"

She saw his mouth moving, but couldn't make out the words.

"Huh?"

He smiled, shaking his head, and motioned for her to roll down the window.

I am such an idiot! Laughing at herself, she rolled down the window.

"Trina, I was just thinking, are you busy?"

"No. Actually, not really."

"Have you ever ridden in a Maserati before?"

She bit her lip, trying to control the smile that was invading her face. *No, but I damn sure want to.*

❧ ❧ ❧ ❧ ❧

"So, where should we go?"

Trina shrugged, trying to keep her grin from becoming a full smile. He had asked her to ride. She knew that it didn't mean anything, the old player in her remembering the rules of the game. But still, it had felt good for a handsome man to invite her to join him. She enjoyed parking her car in the crowded lot and climbing into the low wide car. It felt damn good to watch his eyes take in the full width of her and grin appreciatively as he held her hand and commented on her curly hair. She didn't care where they went.

"Wherever you take me."

Once again, he gazed at her. Then, shaking his head and smiling, he eased the car out of the parking lot.

"Let's go where there are some empty roads. Open this baby up a bit."

"Cool."

He turned the music down, and they rode in silence.

"I hope you don't mind my asking you to ride."

"Not at all."

"Good. I didn't want you to be offended or anything."

"Why would I be offended?"

He looked down at her hand. *The wedding band.* She had allowed herself to forget about it. Temporarily.

He shrugged. "I don't know. I just wasn't sure, now that you're married. But, I always liked being around you."

Trina's breath caught in her throat. Either he was the sincerest man she had ever met or he had game.

"That's sweet."

"No, it's true."

They rode in silence until they reached a huge strip of highway with light traffic.

"Here we go!"

Trina leaned back in the seat and let the power of the automobile captivate her. They sped down the highway, and she laughed, encouraged him to floor it, then closed her eyes and pretended she was flying and floating. Thrilled, Trina released herself in the moment.

She opened her eyes when she felt the car slowing down to normal speed. He was watching her, glancing at her and then at the road.

"What you think?"

"Damn."

"Yep, that's what's up."

They both laughed.

"So, you got some time on your hands, or do I have to get you back?"

Trina shrugged. "I gotta little time, why?"

"Want to get some lunch."

"Definitely."

He turned off the main route onto a side road and followed the road to a burger joint.

Trina waited in the car while he went in. *What am I doing? This is nothing. He is just grown, knows how to have a female friend. Just being friendly. That's all.*

She spotted him with the tray and climbed out of the car. They chose the picnic table in the rear, away from the other customers. She sat on the same side of the table as him, their back to the restaurant, facing the thick grove of trees.

"I love French fries."

"Looks like you love ketchup."

"Yep," she laughed as she squeezed a mound of ketchup onto the tray. "For dipping only. Never pour it all over the fry."

"Uh huh. It's a science, right?" He watched smiling, while she dipped the hot French fry and slowly ate it. "You know, I have always liked you."

"I've always liked you too," Trina said easily, through a mouthful of food.

"Naw," Brian sat the burger on the tray, "I have always wanted you."

Trina sat straight up. *Now that was a little too forward. What was she supposed to say to that?* She looked at the tray of food, the mound of ketchup. Anything to avoid his eyes.

"Didn't you know?"

She slowly glanced up at him. "You had a crush. All boys go through that. I knew you would outgrow it."

"It wasn't a crush."

"Of course it was. What else could it be?"

"I loved you. I was in love…" He smiled, shakily, but his eyes never blinked. "There was nothing I could do about it. But, I loved you."

"Well, it happens to us all. That deep infatuation stuff. Then you don't see the person for a few weeks, forget all about them."

"I didn't forget. I never forgot you. It wasn't just infatuation. I was in love."

He stared at her for a few minutes. She couldn't break away from his gaze. It reminded her of how he used to look at her when she would pick him and Terrance up and escort them to wherever they needed to go. Since she was the older sister, with her own apartment, she was always Terrance's escape route. And she was a loyal sister, willingly ready to take them on their next escapade.

She remembered how he used to look at her, stare at her and become tongue tied in her presence. Even Terrance had joked about it, when Brian wasn't around. She thought it was cute, even funny. She would purposely flirt with him to watch him stutter and blush, watch his caramel-colored skin turn red.

Now she was the one blushing. Her deep brown skin suddenly felt hot as she imagined what his lips tasted like, how she would love to straddle him and feel his rise against her temple. But, she couldn't do that. He was her little brother's friend. *What would he think of me? What if he told?*

"I still am."

Her mouth fell open. He leaned in and kissed her lightly on the forehead, then the tip of her nose. Blood rushed to her

110

temple, warmth flooded between her legs. Her eyelids felt heavy, her mind dizzy. She wanted him. As bizarre as it sounded, she wanted him. But she was married with a child. And she was easily ten years older than him.

"I am not asking you for forever. I know you have... obligations," he whispered. "But we have now."

"And then what? There is too much at stake."

"There is nothing at stake, because this stays between us. We both have something to lose. I just don't want to lose another opportunity to be near you. To make something I thought about daily, come true."

Daily? Imagine that. Even if it wasn't true, his approach felt so romantic and poetic that she hoped he would kiss her again. She didn't want to speak; she wanted to feel the sudden flood of desire overtake her again.

He leaned down, this time landing a light kiss on her neck. The feel of his head between her shoulders and neck made her shudder involuntarily.

"I want to be with you," he said after a long pause. He bit his lip, then leaned in next to her ear and whispered, "Do you want me?"

"Yes," she whispered.

"Tell me that you want me. I need to hear it."

"I want you. Now," she whispered, amazed at how quickly she had lost control.

He kissed her neck again, while his index finger slowly traced a path down the V-neck opening of her shirt and circled the base of her breast. She placed her hand on his leg, her eyes closed. She felt his fingers linger just in front of her for a second, then sighed as she enjoyed the sensation of his finger stroking lightly back and forth across her hardened nipple. Her hand firmly grasped his thigh, running slowly along the ridge of his thigh to his tight rippled stomach. The continuous waves of pleasure from his hand stroking her breast caused a moan to escape, just as he fully grasped her lips with his. His tongue lightly teased hers, in and out, just enough to leave her breathless in anticipation.

The first kisses were slow, lingering and playful. But as the waves of passion continued to flutter through her, the kiss became more passionate, deeper, her mouth wide open.

He lowered his hand from her breast, squeezing her knee then her thigh, before slipping his hand under her skirt. His hands massaged Trina's inner thigh, stopping just at the tip of her panties and rubbing lightly. He pressed against her with his thumb, and Trina moaned softly, leaning into him.

Brian separated himself from her for a moment, glancing around. They were far away from the few customers, their table near a grove of tress and just visible underneath the low swinging branches. He swung one leg over the bench and pulled her into him, her back against his chest, his right arm around her. From afar it appeared that they were sitting close, holding each other. But his left hand reached under her shirt and lightly touched both her breasts. Kissing the back of her neck, he slid his hand into the cup of her bra, firmly cupping her entire breast, rubbing her nipple with his forefinger and thumb. She grasped his thigh firmly again, as she moaned in delight.

"Will you let me make love to you?"

Trina nodded her head, wondering what had happened to her resolve, to her ability to say no. It was the memory of his young raw admiration. She could still see it in his eyes. He thought she was beautiful and she could see a wonderful reflection of herself in him. Brian looked at her like a man in love, when every part of his woman is enhanced, magnified and fulfilling. She wanted to lose herself in that image, in that raw, unadulterated admiration.

"I have waited to make love to you for years," he whispered against the back of her neck, before gently sucking it.

As he kissed her neck, his hand left her breast, gently pressed against her belly, submerging under the waistline of her skirt and panties, and firmly cupping the ridge of her pelvis. She leaned back a little, as a slight shudder passed through her again, and he submerged his hands into the depths of her love. Still sitting sideways, his left arm hidden from view, he massaged and stroked her clitoris, kissing her neck through her moans and gasps, gingerly balancing her frame against his body. She rocked slightly in response to the rhythm of his fingers, plunging deeply inside of her, while his thumb continued to press against her clitoris.

"Do you like that?"

She couldn't answer, couldn't form her mouth to make a plausible statement. His fingers moved expertly around her vagina, in and out of her, then up and down teasing her inner walls and driving her into a delirious state.

His fingers stopped moving and he whispered again, "Do you like that?"

"Don't stop," she muttered.

His fingers continued to stroke in and out of her, his thumb rubbing back and forth and pressing light, until she exploded. Her hand squeezed his thigh, while she tried with all her power not to scream, rather she held on as she felt wave after wave of pleasure wash over her frame. Then, suddenly, she was completely exhausted. She leaned into his chest, while his fingers continued to play in her pussy.

He called her name after a few minutes. She raised her head from his chest, and gazed into his eyes. She hoped he didn't say something that would ruin this moment, ruin this feeling of complete relaxation.

"How do you feel?"

She smiled, shook her head. She wasn't ready to talk yet.

"I have thought about how to please you for years," he whispered.

Trina's eyes opened fully, staring into his. She could see love there, although it frightened her. She wouldn't focus on it, wouldn't acknowledge it. She didn't want to ruin this moment.

Trina had never experienced that before, had never met a man who knew how to apply just the right amount of pressure, who knew how to respond to every movement and gentle rock, to bring her to ecstasy with just his hand. He continued to rub her thighs, her belly, breasts, his hand traveling lightly up and down her clothes. The cold food sat untouched in front of them, but the look in his eyes was ravenous.

"Come home with me," he whispered.

She gladly accepted his invitation.

❧ ❧ ❧ ❧ ❧

The first time, they didn't make it back to his house. Sitting in the Maserati, he continued to rub her body. She wanted to just accept it, to lay there and bask in the attention. But she also wanted to please him, to return some of what she felt. She climbed over the center console and press-fitted her body on top of his, as she pressed the control that lowered the seat.

"Oh gawd," he muttered. The utterance surprised her. For the first time he seemed scared and nervous. She looked deeply into his eyes as she kissed each lip gingerly, then traced the fullness of his lips wither he tongue. He seemed

114

nervous, his eyes staring at her questioningly. At first, she didn't understand it, couldn't figure out how someone so astute could now seem nervous.

"What's wrong?" she whispered, nose to nose with him. "Did I do something?"

"No, its just...." He sighed deeply, and she understood. This meant something to him. This was special. And that tenderness, that admission of weakness spawned the strongest feeling of caring that she had ever felt toward anyone.

"It will be alright," she whispered.

She continued to kiss him, slowly and deeply. He wrapped his arms around her torso, his broad frame enveloping her, his hand resting lightly on the back of her head. With each kiss, she slowly ground her body against him, rocking her pelvis against his, feeling his thick rise through the light gym shorts.

Trina nibbled on his neck, ran her hands up and down the back of his head, and kissed him deeply as she continued her slow, methodic grind. Brian moaned thickly, holding her tightly, his hands resting on her hips as she gyrated slowly in a circular motion over his pelvis.

"Oh gawd," he muttered again, this time closing his eyes and giving himself over to the pressure of her body hovering just over his penis, her hips rotating slowing, her breast rubbing up and down his torso. "I can't take it."

"Shhhh...."

Trina ran her hands down his torso and he raised his hips slightly while she lowered his shorts.

"Condom?"

Brian opened his eyes slowly, seemingly unable to move as Trina planted her knees in the side of the seat and lifted her hips, allowing her to stroke him with both hands. He reached under the seat, and Trina heard a compartment click, and then heard him tear the small packet. Taking it from him, she rolled it onto his penis. Kissing him deeply, she raised her hips and slowly lowered herself onto him, hearing him gasp and then moan. When she had fully consumed him, she resumed kissing him, and gyrating her hips, but barely lifting them.

After a few minutes, her passion took over and she could not contain herself. Leaning completely onto him, her hands on the headrest, she slowly lifted and lowered herself, enjoying the complete fullness of him. Whenever she lowered her self she would gyrate her hips, and slowly grind, rubbing her clitoris against his pelvis. She continued this until they were both lost in the sensuous wave of the motion. He held onto her hips as he climaxed, jerking and grabbing, sighing and moaning.

They lay in the Maserati for a long time, until she was able to peel herself from his arms. He bathed her in kisses, whispered repeated promises of ecstasy and finally, they separated and he drove slowly to his house.

ॐ ॐ ॐ ॐ ॐ

She had washed every inch of her body three times. Her house was spotless. James was due home any second and they had planned to spend to rest of the weekend together before going to pick up the baby. She had looked forward to it before, hoping that she could be clever enough to seduce him, to get him to pay attention and want to make love. Lately, he always seemed so tired. All he spoke of was his obligations at work, the different things he was counting on to make money so that they would be comfortable. But they were already comfortable and Trina was bored. Well, she had been bored, before the last twenty-four hours with Brian.

116

She had left early this morning. Brian took her to her car. They talked forever in the parking lot; about being glad they had found each other and enjoyed each other. Both stated clearly that they had no regrets and this would forever be their secret. Before she left, he kissed her deeply in the early morning light of the parking lot.

Trina hadn't felt a bit of guilt. Not at all. She had enjoyed every minute of Brian and wished the day and night would never end. But, here she stood, waiting for her husband to return, waiting for her mundane life to resume.

"Hey honey."

She hadn't expected the sound of his voice. The deep reliable rich tone brought on the flood of guilt. Her knees actually caved a little bit. *Get it together. There is nothing you can do now. It's over.* Trina hurried downstairs to greet her husband.

"Hi, James. How was your trip?"

"Alright. Did you miss me?"

"Yep. Of course."

"I called all night. You didn't answer."

"Dead battery. Just recharged this morning. Sorry about that."

"Well, I called the house phone too."

"Did you?" Trina picked up his bag and headed for their bedroom. "I don't know how I missed that." She placed the bag on the bed. "I needed a little solitude, anyway, so I didn't have it near me."

He nodded, following her into the room. He observed her closely. "You look nice."

"Thanks," she answered, fluttering past to unpack his bag and place the toiletries in the bathroom.

"I missed you."

Uh oh. It was his tone. The once every blue moon, I want to get it on, tone. *No.* She didn't want to do that. She couldn't have sex with him after making love to Brian every which way for the past twenty-four hours. She wouldn't do it.

"I missed you too," she forced through her teeth, as he moved closer to her for a kiss. She turned her head just as he made contact, landing a peck on her cheek.

"Come here, let me have some."

This is exactly why your ass ain't getting none. James had no romance, no sense of adventure. No foreplay, no excitement. *Just a "let me have some" mentality.*

"I don't feel well, James. I'm sorry." Trina floated out of the room to get the other bags and help him unpack.

∽ ∽ ∽ ∽ ∽

It had been twelve days since her encounter. Trina tried to resume a normal life, but she couldn't. The thought of his touch, his taste, his smell filled her mind constantly, making it impossible to focus on the slightest tasks. She had not made love to James in that time. Nor did she plan to. Although she felt guilty about giving herself to another man, the guilt was caused by her own disappointment that she could no longer consider herself to be the perfect wife. It was not an overwhelming loss for going outside of her marriage. James was so cold, so stiff, that if Trina sought warmth somewhere else she couldn't be blamed.

As Trina returned from her kick boxing class, she noticed that she had a voicemail message on her cell phone. She normally didn't check the voicemail; everyone who knew her knew not to waste their time leaving a message. She checked the caller ID; no name appeared with the number. She kicked off her sneakers and laid across the bed, calling the voicemail. It took a few times to remember the password.

"I miss you. I am sorry. I know I shouldn't do this. But, can we have onemogain?"

She couldn't believe he had left such a message. She could have been busted. *What the hell is he thinking*? But, in the next second she giggled wildly, a euphoric pleasure spread through her body. *He wants to see me again. Be with me again. Hold up, was that a booty call*?

She played the message over and over again, listening to the inflections in his voice. It didn't matter. She wanted to see him again. But when and how? And why. It was only a one-time thing, a perfect opportunity at a perfect time. Anything more would be an affair. And she didn't want an affair. Sneaking out at all times to sneak a few minutes here and there, always risking exposure. It wasn't the lifestyle she wanted. *No, I am not going to be that. Just one more time.*

Checking the yard to make sure James hadn't returned; she called the unidentified number.

"You got my message?"

"What, no hello? No, how are you?"

"Como esta sexy mami," he said in a low voice, making her smile and her heart tingle.

"Esta bien," she smiled. The mere sound of his voice made her inner thighs tingle. Her body was responding and she hadn't been on the phone five minutes.

"So, when can I see you again?"

"I don't know it depends on what you have in mind."

"You. I have in mind."

She sighed deeply, enjoying his voice.

"Tomorrow. I want to have you for lunch."

"Excuse me."

"Over for lunch. Can you come over at lunch time?"

"I don't know."

There was silence for a few minutes, while she weighed the advantages over the risk. Her baby would be in childcare and James would be at work. She could do it, if she were careful.

"Please..." he muttered.

"Yeah. Tomorrow at lunch." Hearing him plead broke any strength she had. She would give this man anything he wanted.

That evening, James asked about her day, planned out the next day's events and expectations. She finished the dishes, nodding and busying herself with cleaning, but her every thought was on Brian.

∾ ∾ ∾ ∾ ∾

The next day he met her at the door, before she could ring the bell. As she reached for the huge knocker, one of the double doors swung open and he pulled her in to him, both arms hugging her close, his tongue exploring her mouth.

She squealed in surprise, but quickly lost herself in the urgency of his passion.

He moved her against the wall and she stood pressed between the cold smooth surface and his hard huge body. His hands slid up and down her torso while he deeply kissed her, tearing away from her mouth and planting kisses around her neck. Her eyes closed, her mouth open, her body felt on fire. His hand easily brushed away the cloth of her blouse, his mouth landing intently on her breast. Kissing and sucking each breast, while massaging the other, she called out his name in pleasure.

"Baby," he moaned. "Say my name again."

And she did, repeating it slowly, while he separated her thighs gently with his knee, submerging his hand into her pussy

120

and massaging it carefully, while landing kisses on her neck. And she continued to call his name, louder, while he cupped her ass with both hands and blew in her ear, sucking lightly on her earlobe. She called his name as she felt him firmly hold her waist and lift her up along the wall, resting her thighs on each shoulder as he pressed his face into the warmth of her vagina. She screamed in delight, rubbing his perfectly shaped head, clinging to the wall for dear life, as he licked and sucked, coaxing her into orgasm after orgasm, encouraging her to release all inhibition and cover him with her natural love.

Exhausted, but still stimulated, he slowly lowered her legs, and she slid effortlessly down his body. He mumbled words of love to her as he laid her gently on the floor and stared into her eyes. She stared back, unable to speak, but also afraid of what she would say. He was turning her out and she knew it, but couldn't stop it.

When he entered her, they both groaned in pleasure, but both kept their eyes locked on one another. She could feel every inch of him, as if her insides were swollen and press fitting against the perfect shape of him. She shouted in pleasure, as he seemed to grow inside of her, while he rocked back and forth forcefully. Pushing back her legs, he adjusted his thrust, contacting her G-spot. She screamed uncontrollably, until her body experiencing an unbelievable spasm, and he finally released, his shouts drowning her out. *This is the best sex I have ever had in my life.*

They lay quietly on the floor. Within a few minutes he lifted her again and carried her to his bedroom. She kept her eyes closed and remained silent. That he could lift her, carry her, like she was the lightest thing in the world, meant everything to her. She wasn't a burden, someone to be overlooked and mistreated when the opportunity arose. He didn't view her as a burden. And now she felt like a beautiful flower blooming.

Trina spent the rest of the afternoon and early that evening wrapped in his arms, listening to the birds outside, enjoying safety and peace. She spent the rest of the afternoon making love and allowing him full access to her mind and body. She was way past a one-night stand, and she no longer had any control.

≈ ≈ ≈ ≈ ≈

"Why didn't you call and tell me dinner was going to be late?"

"Because, James, dinner was the last thing on my mind."

"Well, what is on your mind? It damn sure ain't me or us."

"What?" She placed the pan of baked pork chops on the island. "What the hell is that supposed to mean?"

"It means that I shouldn't have to wait for dinner after a hard days work."

Trina remained silent. *A hard days work, my ass.* How hard was managing other people's money.

"Your damn mind has been somewhere else lately. That's all I am saying. And I don't understand your problem."

"I don't have a problem, James."

"Well, then what's going on with you?"

"Nothing. Maybe the fact that you are just now tuning in, after three years of my requests for a partner in this relationship, leads you to believe something is wrong."

She lowered a plate from the shelf, piling the food onto it.

"I don't need that much food. And don't overreact."

"James, I am not overreacting. I am not being irrational. What I am is completely pissed off that you would have the nerve to criticize me when you act like you don't even know me for weeks at a time."

122

Trina's body ached from the lovemaking escapade earlier that day. She and Brian had been seeing each other at least once a week for the past two months. She couldn't get enough. She knew she was addicted, but didn't want the addiction to end. Brian studied her every movement, her every response and then played her body as if it were a finely tuned instrument. Just the slightest blow from his sweet lips could send her into orgasm.

James actually was the furthest thing from her mind. In fact, she hadn't really thought about him at all. And he noticed.

A small part of her panicked. Trina realized that her comfortable existence was, in large part, due to his efforts. But she also wanted to feel loved and protected and James never did that for her.

"Trina if you don't want to be here, you don't have to," James whispered. "If you don't want me than you can leave. I won't fight you."

Trina stared at him. "Are you threatening me? What are you talking about?"

"No. This is me saying that I am not holding you hostage and I have not done anything for you to treat me the way you do. "

"Yes, you have. You never pay me any attention. All you care about is the bills, your job, getting some sleep—"

"Listen to you. You sound like a spoiled brat. 'Nobody ever treats me like I want,'" he answered, mimicking her with disgust.

Trina stared at the back of his head, wondering whether she should leave him or not. She did not answer. *No, I will stay. I will tolerate you, you selfish bastard. And I will keep the deep love that I have with Brian.* Trina carefully sat the plate on the counter top, slowly removed her apron and walked quietly to her bedroom.

CHLOE R. writes expressive and intimate tales, explaining love, describing lust, inviting the reader's imagination to follow the erotic path wherever she leads. Chloe is currently drafting her first novel, an expansion of her erotic short story *Discovering Love*. Her work is also contained in the anthologies *Mental Seduction: Erotic Escapades Volume I* and *Mocha Chocolate: Taste a Piece of Ecstasy*.

Indecent Proposal

Glowing deep chocolate, with dustings of gold-tone eye shadow and bronze glossy lips, an African porcelain doll—accentuated strong cheekbones that mimicked her African ancestry. In a seductive upsweep, long curly locks adorned her crown. Unruly tendrils lazily fell down around her brow, as if she had just finished making love.

Tall and graceful, a true beauty to behold, Jessica stood at the counter and sipped a cup of piping hot Chocolate Latte. Long piano player fingers wrapped around the Styrofoam cup as the piping hot drink trickled down the back of her throat, warming her insides on a cool summer evening. The current issue of *The Afro American Newspaper* was tucked firmly under her arm. After paying for the Latte, she'd sought out an empty table in the busiest place in town, Starbucks.

Oblivious to all, she sat her purse and newspaper down on the table, before dropping the charcoal snakeskin briefcase to the floor. Sitting, she gracefully crossed one long, curvaceous leg over the other and lightly feathered a loose tendril from her brow. Reaching down, she opened the briefcase, retrieved her laptop, and flipped it open. Patiently waiting for it to warm up, she sipped the near tepid Latte and eyed the small coffee shop that swarmed with fellow caffeine addicts. Abruptly, her eyes froze on the tall figure, whose massive shoulders filled out the tattered denim jacket.

Umph, umph, umph.

Standing tall, straight and towering over everyone around him, he stood as tall as an oak tree, exuding confidence. His large hands made the coffee cup disappear—you know what they say about men with huge hands. She glanced down at his feet.

Lord have mercy.

Feeling awkward staring at him, but unable to redirect her stare elsewhere, her eyes wandered below his waist. His worn denim hugged his delicious ass, delicately caressing the bulge *that probably made up a mound of sweet tasting jewels*, she thought. With a mind of its own, her tongue slipped out of her mouth and stroked her bottom lip. *Absolutely beautiful*, she thought as the twitching of her clitoris made her smile and think dirty thoughts about a stranger.

When he turned in her direction, their eyes met. His smile was warm and inviting, giving her a warm and fuzzy feeling, causing a twitching encore in her panties.

Embarrassed, Jessica looked down at her laptop and closed her eyes. *What an idiot*, she thought. *I might as well hang a sign on my forehead that reads "desperate."*

Startled by the tall figure now towering over her, she quickly, and nervously, closed her laptop.

"Hello" he greeted.

With her head slightly turned away from him, her eyes rolled up toward him. She nearly melted. Stammering over her thoughts, she tried to find something to say that didn't make her sound like the complete idiot she felt like.

"Usually, when someone says hello to you, the courteous response is hello."

"I'm sorry, you're right. You caught me off guard," she smiled sheepishly. "Hello."

"I noticed you are sitting alone. Will someone be joining you?"

Jessica shook her head no. *Aggressive. I likes! Signs of a Leo.*

He smiled and motioned toward the chair. "Do you mind?"

"Please, have a seat."

"Thank you. I'm Angelo and you are?"

Yes you are an angel. "I'm Jessica. Nice to meet you, *Angelo.*" She spoke his name in a flirtatious manner, and with emphasis.

He smiled. "Nice to meet you, Jessica. You're stunning," he said, really pouring it on thick.

"Not today," she responded sarcastically. Just when she thought she had come across a nice guy, he ends up being a corny game player like all the rest.

"Corny, right?"

"Right," she said, resting her chin in her hand, her head tilted to the side. She wondered if he was a mind reader. *Damn, I want to feel you inside of me, can you read that thought?*

"Listen, I'll stop beating around the bush. I believe in being up front, this way there will be no confusion and if you choose you want to roll with it, then cool."

"I beg your pardon? Roll with what?"

"I find you sexy. I want to make love to you."

Jessica broke out in hysterical laughter. "Yes, you're corny *and* full of shit," her laughter pausing, "not to mention rude."

"You obviously find me attractive because your eyes damn near pierced a hole through me."

"You're alright. I mean, you're no Blair Underwood, but you'll do," she chuckled, her eyes freezing on his long, lean form.

Umph, sweetness, deliciousness, and long extremities all wrapped up in the nicest package I've ever seen in my life, hot damn!

127

He was a sight to behold, that's for sure. And that smile, shining brighter than a full moon. She was feeling a little froggish and was wondering what she'd get if she were to leap. *Probably some kind of disease,* she thought. It had been a while since her pussy had been feasted on and she was feeling quite horny. But, he was a stranger, who could've been walking around spreading infectious diseases. However, she'd run down her last two double-A batteries, so her silver bullet was out of commission until she made her weekly visit to Rite Aid.

"So, let me see if I understand what you're proposing. You don't know me from a can of paint and you want to have sex with me?"

"No, I don't want to have sex with you. I want to *make love* to you."

She sipped her now warm Lattè and crossed her legs, tightly. This shit was turning her on. "There's no difference."

"Oh there's a difference between having sex and making love."

"Yes, except you don't love me. So, it would be sex."

"I don't need to love you to *make* love to you. Besides, using the phrase, 'having sex' is so impersonal. Don't you think?"

"Approaching a complete stranger with such an indecent proposal is quite impersonal," she snapped, yet still feeling flattered he chose her to run his bullshit on.

However, there were touches of humor around his mouth and near his eyes that intrigued her. She was actually contemplating his proposal. What in the hell was she thinking?

"So, uh…what do I get in return?" she asked, knowing how stupid the question sounded because she had no intentions, whatsoever, of having sex, making love, fucking, screwing, doing the do, gettin' her groove on, doin' the nasty, sixty-nine, or doing anything else with any stranger. So what if her clit throbbed like a migraine and she could wring the juice from her panties? It wasn't happening.

"What you'll get in return is the best love you've ever had. The kind of love that will have your pussy twitching for days; the kind of love you will want over and over, and the kind of love you won't have to pay for."

Sweet Mother of... "Okay, now you're being rude. I don't think I want to play this game anymore."

"Sure you do."

Jessica stood to her feet. "No, I don't. Now, if you'll excuse me." She grabbed her belongings and headed toward her vehicle. Angelo was quickly on her heels.

Her heart raced rapidly, not from fear, but from the anticipation of giving in to him. She wanted to be with him, *but this was silly*, she thought. She didn't know him. She needed to at least have three dates before she spread eagle for anyone.

Jessica fumbled in her purse for her keys, before dropping them to ground.

Angelo quickly grabbed them and dangled them before her. "Okay, I get it. You're an old-fashioned sister. Would you prefer dinner first?"

"Yes, as a matter of fact, I would prefer dinner, conversation, a few dates an AIDS test and anything else you can think of before you try to fuck me. Oh, my bad, *make love* to me."

"Oooh, feisty, just how I like it."

Jessica snatched her keys from his grasp. "Look, you sicko, you're bothering me."

Angelo took a step backward. "Look, I'm sorry. I'll let you be. I just was...never mind."

When Angelo turned to walk away, Jessica opened her mouth, as if she was going to speak. Then suddenly, her mouth closed and she slid behind the wheel of her spanking new candy apple red Mercedes, drop top. She was interested, but he was coming on a little too strong for her taste. She'd never been approached in such a manner and it made her uncomfortable. *What the hell*, she thought. "Angelo!" she yelled out. "Have you ever heard of foreplay?"

"Yes, I love their music," he smiled. Her apprehension abated somewhat under the warm glow of his smile. The beginning of a smile tipped the corners of her mouth. "You have a beautiful smile," he noticed.

"Thank you. Can we start over?"

His lips curved into a smirk. "I would like that," he said trotting around to the passenger side of her car. "Let's go to my place," he suggested.

"Now see!"

"Just joking," he chuckled, but he was serious. When he first laid eyes on Jessica, his dick hardened like ice and the desire to cool her sexy apple bottom ass overwhelmed him.

"But, I do know of a place where we can go and talk, if you'd like," she offered.

"Sounds good to me."

ৡ ৡ ৡ ৡ ৡ

Jessica inserted the key into her front door. What was she thinking, bringing a complete stranger to her home? "Would you like some coffee?"

"Not unless we're planning on being up all night," he chuckled.

"Well, I don't have any alcohol. I don't drink the hard stuff. But there may be a bottle of wine in the fridge."

"That's cool, I don't need any," he said, following her into the living room, watching and salivating as her voluptuous ass swayed from side to side. He smiled and shook his head with delight. *I will enjoy that sweet ass.*

"Get comfortable," she said, "while I get out of these shoes. My feet are killing me."

Smiling, he stood in the middle of the floor and watched her as she disappeared into the bedroom. He took off his jacket and started to lay it across the sofa, but he quickly changed his mind and draped it across his arm instead. The sofa was white as snow, as well as the other furniture. Her apartment looked more like a showplace than a place to relax, which was making him uncomfortable by the minute. The only splash of color was a huge, beautiful art piece by Charles Bibbs hanging over the sofa. He was really digging her taste, but it didn't feel too homey to him.

"I'll be out in a minute," she yelled from her bedroom. "Help yourself to the fridge."

"Thanks." He draped his jacket over the back of the dining room chair, which was white too, but by this time, he didn't care. *Why have furniture you can't sit on*, he thought, then he slithered into the kitchen and peeked inside the refrigerator. He reached in and pulled out a bottle of wine he'd never heard of before, JazzBerry by Boordy Vineyards. He thought the bottle was interesting, because of its unique label. It was the first time he'd seen a wine bottle with people partying on the label. He shrugged his shoulders and searched the kitchen cabinets for two wine glasses and headed for the dining room, sitting the glasses on the glass-topped dining room table. He peered down at the two white lion statues holding the glass top in place. Something he would've never thought to do, but interesting nonetheless. He popped the cork and partially filled the glasses.

"You have a nice place," he shouted, as he wondered what was taking her so long. He needed to hurry this along because his desire to be intimate with a stranger was beginning to fade. "Are you going to be much longer?"

After a fifteen-minute wait, Jessica finally graced him with her presence. "That wasn't too long, was it?"

"I thought I was going to have to call in the National Guard," he chuckled.

"Yes, well, I had to get myself...uh, in the mood. I've never brought a stranger home before."

"I can dig it," he stated, "but I'm sure you'll have no regrets."

She nervously nodded toward the glasses sitting on the table. "I see you found the wine," she smiled.

"Yes, I hope you don't mind. I thought we both could use a glass...to unwind."

She reached for the glass of wine before he could do the honors. With the glass pressed against her lips, she flung her head back as the red liquid vanished down her throat. He looked at her in astonishment. She extended the glass toward him. As he began to pour, she said, "To the rim, please."

His eyes left the glass and darted at her. *Not a damn lush*. He wasn't interested in a woman who had to drink to get herself in the mood. But then again, considering the fact she didn't know him from a head of lettuce, it could be overlooked.

After two more full-to-the-rim glasses of wine, Jessica inhaled and exhaled, followed by a long sigh. "Well, are you ready?"

"Ready for what?"

"Ready to love me."

He glared into her eyes. They were quite glossy, reminiscent of a drunkard. Now, his desire was null and he was no longer interested. But, he'd come this far; he was going to see it through. "How about a little music?"

"Sure, what's your pleasure?"

"Something soft."

I can give you diamonds, Alicia Keys belted out.

"I really love this song," she said. "Hell, I love all of her songs."

"The sister is very talented, and attractive to boot."

Her eyes roamed the room. "Listen, can we get this over with?"

Impatient, and nervous as hell. "What's the rush?"

"I'm not rushing," she said, switching her weight from one side to the other. "It's getting late."

"Sweetie, it's only eight o'clock." He took a step closer and grabbed her hands and caressed them. "We have all night." He cupped her face and pulled her into him. His lips brushed against hers. The hairs on the back of her neck stood to attention. Every muscle in her body tensed, she became frigid. When he kissed her eyelids and said, "Relax, baby," the tense lines on her face disappeared and her body relaxed in his arms. He grabbed her by the waist, pulled her closer and gently rocked her from side to side, his hips slowly gyrating his abdomen against hers. His hardened staff poked her. She slightly moaned. Gently kissing her, he slid his hand under her blouse and cupped her breast. Her body stiffened from his touch, as the throb between her thighs intensified. She flinched at every caress and pinch he made on her half-dollar nipples. She couldn't control the spasmodic trembling within her.

With a swift motion, her blouse eased over her head and billowed to the floor. He removed her bra and knelt down before her. He unzipped her skirt and it fell down around her freshly manicured toes. He stroked her nipples with his tongue and then trailed down to her chocolate cove and lightly blew. A delightful shiver of her wanting him ran through her. He slithered his tongue through her opening and instantly became intoxicated as he tasted her essence.

She felt the blood surge from the top of her head to the tips of her toes. Her body heaved, her breast jutting upward as his finger entered through her juices, connecting with her swollen bud.

She raised her arms above her head and stretched. "Oooh," she cooed, causing his shaft to fight with his pants, desperately needing to break free and nestle between her thighs, in the warmth and wetness of her sweet love. "That feels so good, Angelo." She moved her hips in a slow, circular motion. "Hmmm," she moaned, "baby, damn!"

For six months, Jessica had been experiencing menopause and her desire for sex had gone down the drain, so she had thought. But, thanks to Angelo, she was restored and her ass was on fire, a raging inferno.

Angelo looked up at her. "Sweet baby, come down here," he said, pulling her down to his side. "Kiss it for me." She leaned into his abdomen and puckered her full heart-shaped lips. She inhaled and smiled to herself. Angelo smelled refreshing. As she kissed the head of his love, he placed his hand on the back of her head. His head fell backward. His heart jolted and his pulse quickened as she took him in to the back of her throat. "Damn, woman," he moaned.

He laid back on the floor and pulled her on top of him. "Wait one second," she whispered. "I'll be right back." She darted for the bedroom and returned with a condom. Using her teeth, she tore open the silver package and pulled out the condom, tossing the wrapper across the room. She placed the condom on the tip of his head and slowly rolled it down and over his extremely hardened shaft. *What a beautiful dick.* She leaned down and kissed him. Then, she slightly raised her hips and lowered herself down onto him. He flinched; it felt so good and tired. His hands slowly moved downward, skimming either side of her body to her thighs, down to the opening of her lips, searching for her pleasure points. He continuously flicked her swollen bud with his finger, as her hips pumped up and down, her pussy speaking to his dick each time her lips touched his abdomen.

Intensely, he gazed into her eyes. "Fuck your dick, baby. Take that shit."

She threw her head back. "Yes!" she released a deep-throated moan.

"Damn, girl, shit you've got some good ass pussy. I knew your shit was good when I saw your ass. Fuck me, Ma!"

She wasn't used to so much nasty talking during sex and it was turning her on. The sexual groove of her hips quickened, as her clit stroked against his tool, causing enough friction to start a serious forest fire. "Call me bitch," she ordered, gazing into his eyes, with a look he'd never seen before.

"Fuck me, bitch!"

"Slap my ass, motherfucker."

The sting from the palm of his hand sent her to an all new high. Pulling herself up, she grabbed hold of his chest and squeezed as hard as she could, holding on as she rode the fuck out of her buck.

"Oh shit, I'm about to come!" she yelled, fucking him faster.

"Come on, baby, fuck me. Yeah, bitch, that's what I'm talking about."

Grabbing hold to her hips, he pumped up against her, meeting her with each quick stroke, until she couldn't hold it anymore. A wave of pleasure crashed through her, as she exploded all over the dick that nutted profusely.

Exhausted, Jessica lay beside Angelo as he leaned over and, with his tongue, stroked her hardened nipple, down to her opening. Without thought, she spread her legs and wrapped them around his neck. He nestled his face in her cave and feasted on her juices, drinking himself into a euphoric stupor.

MARY WOODS is the alter ego of a well-known best-selling author.

Pushed Beyond Limit

Simone's long, muscular leg stretched over his shoulder as he slid deeper into the depth of her love. "You can do better than that!" she screamed, "Come on, fuck me!"

Troy fucked her mechanically, a machine bent on beating her pussy into submission. Over and over, he slammed into her, his breath coming in hot blasts against her face, as he grunted in time with each thrust. A pool of sweat danced on his forehead and dripped onto her firm, erect nipples.

"Harder, Troy, fuck me harder!"

Like Paul Bunyan, he drove his tool deeper into her canyon, pumping deep into her a few more times, as his chocolate balls slapped against her ass.

"Come on, motherfucker!" Forcefully, she pushed her hips into him, making him drive deeper and deeper, pounding against the reddish-pink cushiony walls of her sex.

His energy draining, loving her was no longer pleasurable. Instead, it felt like pulling a sixteen-hour shift.

Distorted was her face, and scary, like a Vampire ready to sink her fangs deep into his neck, draining him of all blood rushing to the tip of his mushroom head shaped dick. "Are you going to work this pussy or what?"

Drenched in sweat, dripping down onto her face, rolling down her cheeks and onto her chest, Troy showed signs of reaching his breaking point.

She teasingly chuckled. "You need to act like you want this pussy, shit! I know bitches that'll eat my pussy better than you fuck it."

Rage building inside him, as she wrapped her shapely legs tightly around his waist, Troy fucked her as hard as he could. If she survived that night, she would be black and blue the next day. Even worse, her pussy was drying and the friction of his dick, against her dry lips, was about to cause a forest fire, but she did not care. At the moment, she wanted to feel him drilling up into her stomach, if only he would fuck her deep enough. Shit, she couldn't feel it and she was sick of it. She had been casually fucking Troy for six months, and never had an orgasm by penetration, always by oral stimulation.

Even though Troy's dick was bringing her closer and closer to the edge, she would not let him push her over, not wanting the drilling of his dick into her hole to end. She bit down on her bottom lip, trying not to come. The harder he fucked her, the harder she bit down until the taste of blood rested on her tongue.

"Call me bitch, motherfucker, call me bitch!" she yelled, her legs affixed firmly around his waist, limiting his ability to move, with precision, in and out of her dry cunt.

His deep-stroking rhythm came to an abrupt halt. "Bitch, will you *shut* the fuck up?"

"Yeah, baby, that's what I'm talking about," she cooed, stroking his bottom lip with her tongue. "Don't stop fucking me."

"Shut the fuck up!" In a huff, he rolled off her and onto his back. "You run your mouth too goddamn much, woman. How in

138

the fuck am I supposed to concentrate if you keep running your fucking mouth?"

Leaning up on her elbow, she stroked his chest, twisted his curly hair around her fingers, before moving over his stomach, down toward his abdomen, and finally wrapping the palm of her hand around the shaft of his rod.

Moving downward and positioning herself between his legs, she smiled up at him and said, "That's your problem, baby, you concentrate too much. Just go with the flow."

His head buried deep into the pillow, as her hand stroked his dick, easing the built up tension. "Suck it for me, boo," he said, grabbing her by the head and pushing his dick between her full luscious lips.

Simone took as much of him as she could. As his dick stroked the back of her throat, she tried to suppress the urge to heave. Closing her eyes tightly, she concentrated on the task at hand—making her man come, and praying for him to return the favor. The thickness of him was choking her, but he kept pushing up, more and more, into her mouth, his hand holding tight to the back of her head. She grabbed at his jewel sacks, trying to get him to slow his roll, but it wasn't happening.

"Get it good and wet," he said.

She did as he said, moistening the length of him with her mouth until his shaft glistened. She was hoping she could make him come just from sucking him, and tried to keep him in her throat. However, as Simone thought he would lose it, he pulled her off his dick.

Flipping her onto her back, Troy mounted his pony and entered with ease. As he began to ride her fluidly, with long deep intensified strides, his tongue flickered in and out of her mouth, tasting her lips, then moving over to her earlobe,

139

twirling around her spot, causing her to push into him, as her clitoris stroked rapidly against his hardened shaft.

As her legs wrapped tight around his waist, she pulled him into her. Troy, slowly, yet precisely, deep stroked her pussy, rubbing against her sweet spot—that tiny knot on the ceiling of her cave.

"Ooo, sweet baby," she cooed, unwrapping her legs, raising them in the air and spreading them wide, her pussy swallowed him completely, his chocolate jewels tapping a rhythmic beat, like a Congo drum, against her ass.

"Baby, you gotta fuck me, shit," she sensuously cried, pounding her hips into him. "Come on tear this ass up, nigga."

"Hush," he whispered in her ear, as beads of sweat poured off him and onto her forehead, glistening like tiny diamonds.

"Baby, fuck me in the ass," she said, twirling her tongue in circles beneath his earlobe.

"Say what?" he panted, with deep breaths, borderlining exhaustion.

"I wanna feel you in my ass."

Troy ceased stroking. "You trippin' now, Simone. You know I don't do that shit."

She kissed his lips. "I think we should try different things."

"Yeah, okay." Again, he rolled off her and onto his back. "If I remember correctly, the last time I mentioned your asshole, you called me a fuckin' fag."

"We had just gotten together then, this is now— me and you."

"Naw, and you messed up my flow with that shit too."

"Well, damn baby, I need to feel some type of penetra–" She caught herself, but it was too late. His ego had already hit the floor, while his anger rose to higher plains.

Troy looked at her sharply and pursed his lips together. "What was that?" His body stiffened. Closing his eyes, he clenched his mouth tight. Her venomous mouth had spewed the ultimate poison. "Get out," he mumbled. Inhaling deeply, trying to calm the shaking caused by the massive blow incurred from Simone's sharp tongue, Troy's eyes met hers despairingly. "You need to raise up outta here."

She rose up on her elbows and leaned into him. "I'm sorry, Troy. I didn't mean that, baby. You know that."

"Yeah, you meant it," he whispered. "You have a tendency of coming out your mouth half-assed."

"No, I didn't. Honest, baby, I didn't mean it. I guess, I just got caught up in the moment."

"Whatever, you need to get the fuck out, for real."

"But, baby–"

"Goddamn, get the fuck out, bitch!" Pushed to the limit, beyond the point of being irate with her, he felt the pulsating veins in his neck, ready to pop. And, if Simone did not make her move, quick fast and in a hurry, she may end up receiving unwanted assistance.

Simone leaped to her feet. Standing before him, as her cream oozed down her thighs, her hands propped on her hips, the sister-gurl head roll began, as she pointed her finger in his face. "Why do I have to be a bitch?" Speaking softly, almost in slow motion, she said, "You little dick motherfucker?" Pacing the floor, she continued. "If your dick had any length or girth, I wouldn't be crying for you to go deep so I could feel that little shit; the size of a baby's bottle nipple. Who do you think you are, treating me like this?"

He pulled himself out of bed and walked toward the window. He turned his back on her and gazed out into the traffic briskly moving up and down Baltimore Avenue.

She exuded a contemptuous laugh. "Your dick is too fucking small!" She continued teasing, wanting to get the best of him, refusing to allow him to have the last word. "No matter how much I suck, pull and tug at it, it doesn't get any harder. Face it, Troy, you're over forty and smack dead in the middle of the limp noodle stage. Ever thought about Viagra?"

Troy cringed at her words and hoped she would gather her things quickly, before he would have to introduce her ass to his foot. His boys told him about fucking with a twenty-something chickenhead, but he listened to the mid-life crisis phase that had taken over his common sense.

Walking up behind him, she continued chiding at him. "Yeah, motherfucker, I don't need you to fuck me. Shit, I know plenty of niggas whose dick I can feel and–"

SLAP!

Simone didn't know what hit her.

Swiftly, the back of his hand landed across her mouth, sending her flying against the wall, where she leaned on shaky legs, in shock.

He's in shock too. He'd never struck a woman a day in his life. "Baby, I'm sorry...I don't know what came over me," he said apologetically.

"Yeah, you sorry, all right. You are one sorry ass motherfucker!" she cried, pulling herself off the wall, trying to stand steady on her own two feet.

Troy lowered his head and massaged his forehead before staring her straight in the eyes. His jaws flinched and flickered. "You ain't tight anymore."

A look of confusion danced across her face, as she forced a smile. But, for real, she was not confused. She knew exactly what he meant, her legs had been an automatic door for the past seven days, fucking every man who winked at her. "What?"

Troy shifted his weight and rested his hands on his hips. "Your pussy," he said, his hand waving in the air, "…it ain't tight. Stretched wide…almost like a Mack truck drove through your shit. And, it don't smell nice…almost like some other nigga."

"What are you insinuating, *Troy*?"

"I'm not the only one you been fucking, *Simone*."

"I have not been fucking around on you! How dare you accuse me of–"

"For once, Simone, be honest with me, damn it!"

"Troy, I haven't been with anyone else," she lied, "you have to believe me. I love you too much, I would never, ever give my love to anyone else."

Troy gathered Simone's clothing and shoved them into her arms. "No? Well, you smell like some other nigga. And why all of a sudden you're into this hard, rough sex? We've never fucked like that before. You know it's not my style."

"I…I don't want us to be inhibited, that's all. Do different things. And I told you I ain't been with nobody else."

He didn't believe her bullshit for a minute. He grabbed her by the arm, as she struggled to break free of his grasp, and escorted her to the front door.

"Troy, at least let me put my clothes on," she whined.

Troy opened the door and shoved her into the hallway. "Put your clothes on out there," he growled, slamming the door in her face.

Banging on the door, with her fist, Simone cried, "Troy, you can't do me like this!"

Opening the door, Troy gazed at her. If looks could kill…He grabbed his dick and aimed it at her. "You ain't worth a shit," he said, aiming a stream of piss that splashed off her tight abdomen. Exuding a hearty laugh, "You dirty bitch, get out my life," he said slamming the door in her face.

Troy shook the remaining droplets off his dick where they landed on the floor, and walked over to the window, where he pulled the curtain back and watched Simone stumbling to dress before sliding into the 2002 Nissan Maxima XE that he gave her for her birthday.

"I'll have that shit repo'd tomorrow," he snarled.

JESSICA TILLES is an award-winning, critically-aclaimed author, publisher, founder, and CEO of Xpress Yourself Publishing, LLC, Poetic Press (an Xpress Yourself Publishing imprint) and The Writer's Assistant. A native of Washington, DC, she is a creative writer in all genres of fiction, with several titles in print: *Anything Goes, In My Sisters' Corner, Apple Tree, Sweet Revenge, Fatal Desire, Unfinished Business* and *Erogenous Zone: A Sexyal Voyage* (an anthology). Jessica is the recipient of the 2003 Memphis Black Writer's Conference's Rising Star Award for Literature and The Jackson Mississippi Readers Club's Contribution to African American Literature Award.

My Dream Come True

I could blame it on that third Margarita but even I knew better. The tequila just gave me that extra kick of courage I needed to say and do what I was too timid to do and say in my sober state. As the smooth frozen liquid slid down my throat, I could feel the adrenaline pumping in my veins. I started feeling the music and before I knew it, I was on top of the table, gyrating my wide hips, as I seductively rubbed my thighs.

My girlfriends cheered me on. It was my birthday and they brought me out to the club to celebrate turning thirty. I wanted a simple, conservative dinner at Red Lobster but my girls wouldn't hear of it.

"You've got to come out of that shell!" Monica had said. "How will you ever find a man, if you're always shut inside?"

"And when she does come out, she's always got on a turtleneck and oversized dress pants." That was Amber. "Zora, you've got to loosen up! We're taking you shopping and then we're going over to Club Desire!"

I had protested but to no avail. They hauled me off to the mall and bought me clothes that I never would have selected for myself. I didn't even feel comfortable stepping out of the dressing room because the clothes were so revealing. But, I had to admit that I was looking hot. Wearing clothes in a size seven gave new life to my curves that were usually hidden under the size elevens I wore. I eventually gave in and thanked them for the new wardrobe.

Our next stop was Sandi's. For years I had worn my hair in nothing more than a ponytail and a bang, that I trimmed myself. My girls insisted that I get myself a 'real' hairstyle. Fighting with them was pointless. I sat back in the chair, with my eyes closed, as Sandi trimmed away layers of my naturally sandy colored hair.

"You look like a new person!" she exclaimed when she was done. "You were already pretty but now you're gorgeous!" That said, I opened my eyes and stared in the mirror at my reflection. Only it wasn't me. At least, it wasn't the same *me* I had seen staring back at me for thirty years. This me sported a neatly trimmed wrap that hugged my pear shaped face. I had to agree. I was definitely looking good.

After the new do, my girls took me back to my place. Monica gave me a manicure and a pedicure. Both were well overdue. Amber gave me a facial that left my skin feeling light and tingly. She then applied a thin layer of makeup to my copper-colored face. I was in awe when I looked in the mirror and saw the runway model staring back at me. My girls had hooked me up!

Now I feel masculine arms around my small waist. I open my eyes and stare down at the man lifting me into his arms and off the table. He's jet black and his eyes are a deep brown. He's tall and slender. Something in his eyes and his smile tell me not to fear him. So, I don't. I throw my arms around him as I continue my dance. I grind my hot body against him as he stares deeply into my eyes. He never blinks and his smile never fades.

"I think you've had one drink too many." When he finally speaks, his voice is deep and seductive. At least he's seducing me. I don't know if he means to but he is.

"I just wanna dance." I can't help but giggle as I hear the slurred words leave my lips. From my lips to his ears; even he laughs.

"Maybe you guys should take her home." It's the last thing I remember hearing before passing out.

At home, I awake in my bed, unclothed, to find this stranger kneeling over me. His soft kisses awakened me from my drunken slumber.

"Hey, Beautiful," he whispers as he plants a kiss on my nose. The sensation sends chills up my spine. His lips are soft and full.

I don't say anything. I pull his face to mine and press my lips against his. Our mouths open and our tongues unite in a dance of tug of war. It's only the second time I've kissed a man. And this is much better than kissing Tyron Brown, in Monica's closet, on her thirteenth birthday. I only kissed him because we were playing spin the bottle and his spin of the bottle landed on me. Neither of us wanted to kiss. He was in love with Monica and my father had warned me about kissing boys. So, we just closed our eyes, counted to three, and pressed our lips together for about a half of second. He ended up getting his chance with Monica and I promised myself that I would never disobey my father again.

Our heated kiss led to tender caresses. His strong hands fondled my ample breasts. The heat in my loins was rising and I could feel moisture at the entrance of my virginity. I had vowed to wait until marriage before having sex. My father, Reverend Leroy Anderson, had raised his only daughter to be a lady and being a lady meant sharing myself with only one man, my husband. Rarely dating made it hard to find a husband.

"I want you," the man, whom I didn't even know by name, whispered as he nibbled on my ear. I wanted him, too. I wanted to know what it felt like to have a man fill my hole of lust. For years, I had wondered how it would feel to reach orgasm that was brought on by something other than my own fingers. My girls talked about it all the time and I wanted to have something to say on the subject as well.

I lie back on the bed and spread my legs wide open. I was going to give him what we both wanted. My body ached for it and craved it. There was a pounding in my heart and inside my tight walls. Only one thing could satisfy me now. That one thing was the handsome stranger who was now smiling as I rubbed my clitoris with one hand and motioned him to me with the other.

Having never gone this far before, I didn't know what I expected. I know I didn't expect him to bury his baldhead between my open thighs. I didn't expect to feel the heat from his mouth as his tongue stroked my clit. No, it wasn't what I expected but I damn sure enjoyed it! Within minutes, I was experiencing my first *real* orgasm and it was only the beginning.

Oh My! is the name I gave the stranger; he was gentle when he entered me. As wet as I was after my first orgasm, it still hurt so good when he finally pushed his nine, thick inches of manhood inside me. I knew how good Stella felt in the shower because I, too, had a single tear fall from my eyes when he hit my spot and my walls squeezed him ever so tightly as my body exploded once again. This time his body shuddered and together we experienced pure ecstasy.

When I woke up again he was gone. There was not a trace of him. I couldn't even smell the expensive cologne that oozed from his pores or the sweet musk that hung in the air after our lovemaking. I was alone. The man who had brought me to orgasm had vanished into thin air. I opened my mouth to call out to him but quickly remembered that I still didn't know his name. Then I searched for a note or at least some trace of him but found nothing. It had been a dream. But just how much of it did I dream? Did I really go to the club with my girls?

I jumped from the bed and made my way over to the full-length mirror. I was still dressed in the short, red dress. My hair, though disheveled, was still hugging my face. I could still see traces of my lipstick and my nails were still fire hydrant red.

I quickly grabbed my head. It was pounding. The makeover, the club, and the drinks had not been a dream. But, what about *Oh My!*, had he actually lifted me into his arms and stared into my eyes? Did he come to my home and deflower me?

There was a gentle knock at my bedroom door. I smoothed my hair down with my fingers before saying, "Come in!"

It was Amber. "I wanted to check on you. You were pretty wasted last night."

It was Saturday morning and she was dressed casually in a pair of Capris and a tank top that was cut just low enough to reveal her cleavage. Like me, Amber was single.

Unlike me, she was not conservative. She had been married for a short time but was now divorced. We share a two-bedroom apartment.

"I'm okay," I said with a shrug of my shoulders as I tried to ignore the throbbing pain in my head. "H-how d-did I get here?" I had to know for sure that my dream had only been a dream.

"Monica and I brought you home. The bouncer politely threw us out after your table dance." She paused long enough to giggle. "He was nice though. After you passed out, he carried you to Monica's car and helped us strap you in."

"So, h-he didn't come here?" Amber gave me a strange look. "I just wondered how I got to bed. I can't see you and Monica carrying me." I tried to play off her suspicious look with a little joke.

"Well, it wasn't easy but we got you here." She then reached into her pocket and took out a business card. "Marc asked me to give this to you when you sobered up."

I took the card. Before I could ask the obvious she answered, "He's the bouncer from the club. I think he's feeling you." She winked her eye and said, "I think you should call him." She closed the door before I could say a word.

"Marc Grey," I read aloud from the card. He was a landscaper. I wanted to call him. Oh how I wanted that dream to be a part of my reality. I wanted to feel his warm breath as his tongue explored my womanhood. I wanted to be like Stella and have that single tear roll down my cheek because the painful pleasure hurt so damn good.

But, I had promised my father. I had promised him years ago that I would save myself for marriage. Marc didn't look like a man who would be patient enough to wait.

He probably wasn't even looking for a wife. How could I even hope to find a good man in a place like Club Desires? With that thought, I tossed his card aside and went to my private bath to take a long, hot bubble bath.

"Well, did you call him?" Amber, Monica, and I were now outside on the patio having sliced fruit. They were drinking white wine and I was drinking carbonated water. No more alcohol for me. I still had a dull pain in my head from my alcohol buzz last night.

"No. I don't think he's right for me." I said without making eye contact. I taught Bible studies on Tuesdays and sang in the choir on Sundays. I was a mentor to the single, female youth in the church. He on the other hand was a landscaper by day and a bouncer by night. He probably had tons of women that he slept with.

150

"Who would have thought Tyron was right for me all those years ago?" Monica said. It had taken years before she gave into his advances but in our senior year of high school she finally surrendered. It was hilarious to see them together. She was the wild cheerleader and he was the brainy Chess club president. They were not the likely pair.

But somehow they pulled it off and now they're happily married with twin daughters who look like mommy and excel academically like daddy. "But, I just threw caution to the wind and gave him and myself a chance. I don't regret it either."

"And everybody thought that Craig was perfect." Amber spoke of her ex-husband. "He even had me fooled for years. He was smart, good looking, and God fearing. Well, at least that's how he presented himself." She laughed a little to herself and we both reached out to her. She and Craig had only been divorced about a year now and we both knew that he had really broken her heart. "Yep, I thought he was right for me until I caught him in his office with his twenty-year-old, blonde secretary. She had his dick in a lip lock and he was enjoying every second of it. He married that skanky whore before the ink was even dry on our divorce papers. And now she's pregnant with his child even though he kept telling me to wait before we started a family." She was fighting back tears as she relived the painful memories. "But, my point is, things are not always what they seem to be. You just have to get to know people. And sometimes your heart gets broken."

After listening to my friends I decided to give Marc a call. I learned that he was single and had never been married. He didn't have any kids. I even found out that he was a man of God even though he wasn't a member of any one church. He visited different churches every Sunday. Unlike me, he wasn't a virgin but he had been abstinent for five years.

151

"The woman you met at the club, that's not how I usually am," I explained. I went on to tell him about the real me. I told him how much I love working in the church and singing in the choir. I confessed that I was a virgin and would remain that way until I was married.

"It sounds like you're the woman my heart has been searching for." His soft-spoken words brought a smile to my face. "I'm at the club to supplement my income because I'm trying to buy a house in the country. When I find the right woman I want to have a home waiting for her."

And that's how our story began. I gave him and myself a chance and God gave us happily ever after. He's been making that erotic dream come true every night for two years.

SUNSHINE ROYAL resides in South Georgia. She is the mother of two and has been happily married for eight plus years. The writer works full time as a 911 dispatcher but loves to read and write every chance she gets. Please read excerpts from this author's works on her blogs www.myspace.com/linherman.

Grab My Dreads

Fuck James, Todd, D'Angelo, and Rusty. Fuck 'em all. And I mean that shit, straight from the bottom. One dead-end romance after another, same shit, different sorry ass man. I gave my heart, soul, life, body and spirit to these foolish ass brothers, and what do I get in return? A broken heart, lonely nights, and a tight, anxious, need-to-be-dusted-off pussy.

So, who's really the foolish one?

I'm a fine woman, rich in spirit, successful according to my measurement of success, in decent shape, I wear my own hair, no bunions, funyons, or corns on my feet, I got straight teeth, rich honey skin, and I'm clean. Could anyone ask for more? I guess they can, and they do.

Placing the tablespoon of Breyers Natural Vanilla in my mouth, my phone rings. Damnit! I'm right in the middle of watching a rerun of *Martin*. This better be good; taking me out of my comfort zone this gotdamn late.

"Hello?" I snarl into the receiver hoping to turn off whoever it is on the other end of my phone.

"Hey, sweetheart. I miss you," Todd whispers to me sounding like he has his hand on his dick, Vaseline and towel in tow and just needs a sweet voice to take him there. Well, it won't be me, not tonight. I done cried over his ass too many times, and

153

I simply refuse to be taken for granted again by him. By any man for that matter.

"What do you want Todd?" I'm trying to get my point across that I don't have time tonight. Not even if my pussy is screaming, *"what the fuck is wrong with you, Lisa?"*

Todd was no different from the rest of them. They all loved my independence, my self-reliance, the money, the comfort, and the fact that I provided damn near everything. Blessed with world class ass and looks to match, I was a good girl, still am, they knew it, abused it, and never thought they'd lose it. Well, guess what? *It's lost.* Shit, I'm cured of the "disease to please" and have moved on to glory days.

"I want you, Lisa. Tonight. Right now. Please. Let me come over," he says sounding pitiful, sexy, pathetic and succulent all at the same time. Yeah I bet he does want to come over...literally, just dying to release his jism all over my tits like he used to back in the day when I was a dick-whipped-like-butter fool.

"Not tonight Todd, I told you its over." I hang up the phone, wishing like hell I hadn't because the kitty is purring, and in need of some loving, badly, in desperate need of petting and pampering. Damn, I feel my clit throbbing already. I'll be humping the pillow tonight, making love to it as if its name was Denzel.

On the bright side of things, life isn't all that bad. My law practice is growing, although I'm a solo practitioner. And, I'm leaving in two days for a much needed vacation to Montego Bay with my two best friends, Regina and Paula, for a week of fun and to celebrate my thirty-fifth birthday!

The Morning Of...

"Girl, we're going to have a good time this week," Paula says to me with a cheesy ass grin on her face with what appears to be a pair of huge Chips sunglasses on her caramel-coated face.

"I know we will. I am so looking forward to getting a much deserved mental health break," I say to her and glance over to Regina, who is ignoring us, and is focused solely on getting on this airplane. She's acting like the plane is going to take off and leave us here!

Its seventy-thirty in the morning on a Saturday that makes it seem like it's around five a.m. But you won't here a complaint out of me as I will politely and gratefully stand my ass in yet another line here at Newark International Airport, going through more security checks and metal detectors than I do when I walk into a courthouse. This shit kills me; we protect our airports more than a black man on the street. Damn, can't drink a bottle of water in the airport, but my father could get shot to death less than thirty minutes from here. Nevertheless, I'm so ecstatic about going on my first cruise!

"I can't wait to put these rusty feet in someone's hands for a good pedicure!" Regina tells me as we are just about to land in Miami.

"Yes, girl, I've already visualized the massage in my mind, along with the mud bath, manicure and pedicure and the hot cup of green tea afterwards," I say as I open the overhead compartment to grab my bag.

"And don't forget about the ding-a-ling we'll be riding too, ladies," Paula says as we make our way off the plane. The rest of the passengers stare at the three of us in disbelief after Paula's outrageous statement. Regina and I give her the "no you didn't" look and, as if on cue, she boldly exclaims, "Yes, I did!" We all laugh and make our way to baggage claim.

The cab driver bores us with meaningless conversation on our ride over to the ship. He shoots the breeze about how he can't get his new business off the ground, because he has to work so much. John, I think his name is, appears to have come straight from Haiti, and seems nice enough, so I indulge.

"So, John, what part of Haiti are you from?"

"Port of Prince. Why do you ask?"

"I ask because my mother is Haitian and Puerto Rican."

"Is that right? That's why you're so beautiful, eh?"

He glances in his rearview to get another glimpse of me.

I blush.

"Thank you, John."

Regina and Paula are laughing and trying to play it off, and of course, I'm cool as a fan.

Finally, we arrive shipside and John unloads the cab. We tip him, and wait for the ship's crew to come and greet us when the Earth beneath me moves, alters, transforms, and rotates off its axis. Damn, I'm dizzy, shot out, trippin', anxious, shit I'm hot.

My eyes follow his every move as he walks toward us, slowly, or maybe he's just so fly that he walks in slow motion— the confidence in his stride, the slight limp in his oh so sexy swagger convinces me that my immediate assumption may be right—his dick does effortlessly flow to his knees. *My God.*

He is a serious combination of both Heaven and Hell, good and evil, hot and ice cold, a sin and a damn shame, a towering inferno of lust walking my way. The fire in his eyes melts my insides, sets fire to my pussy walls—I'm hot, wet, drenched already, and he's only been in my life for ten seconds. *Damn.*

"Hello, ladies."

We all give each other a "Gotdamn" look and respond in unison. "Hello!"

"May I have your cabin numbers, please?"

"We're in cabin M212," Paula says while tossing her finger between her and Regina.

They decided to split an interior cabin. Since I need a little more space, and because I knew that I'd be bringing some work with me, I decided to get a cabin of my own.

Sweet ass, I mean, the gentleman from the ship approaches me, moving in real close, deliciously invading all of my space and says, "What about you, Miss?"

Damn, he smells like a divine combination of sweat and Cool Water.

"I'm in cabin M214."

"Very well then, ladies. You go aboard now and enjoy your stay with us. I'll have your bags brought to your cabins."

We take the elevator to the Placido deck, where we are greeted with Apple Martinis and the music pumpin' is something fierce. Regina and Paula turn to me, put their glasses up to make a toast and exclaim, "Happy Birthday!" I smile and we get our drink on.

Sitting poolside, we order drinks for the next few hours, while admiring the rich blue skies, the subtle rocking of the boat, the fresh smell of sea air, before deciding to go to our cabins for a nap. The travel time, combined with the drinks, beating sunlight and motions from the ocean have kicked our asses and we need to rest for a minute. We all agree that we'll get dressed for dinner around seven which gives us a few hours to get some sleep.

Can't get ebony majesty out of my mind.

The Princess Room on the main deck is built for kings and queens it seems. It's so regal in here. Chandeliers to die for hang so eloquently from the massive ceilings, while wall to wall carpet, pink walls to offset, and candlelit tables adorning create such ambiance, such magnificence—it's breathtaking.

The many faces of color matching the many jobs make me proud to witness my people, the extensions of my people in such positions. Some are working the bar, while others are serving the food, and others are serving as hosts and hostesses.

Sister girl, with her blonde twists and black form-fitting evening gown escorts us to an available table and lets us know that our server will be with us soon. I already know I'm having the prime rib, and Regina will undoubtedly order the lobster since she doesn't eat red meat, with her anorexic buns of steel self, and Paula, if I know my girl, the way I think I know her, she'll be going for something Italian.

The waiter brings our meals and we enjoy them, talk shit for almost an hour, order a few more drinks when my heart threatens to jump out of my chest as goose bumps form on every skin cell on my entire being. Breathe easy.

Chocolate-dipped passion in male form walks past me, which seems to be in slow motion, and I follow his every move, trying hard as hell not to blink so that I won't miss a thing. He is passion, love, lust on fire wearing a crush linen white pant suit which sets so beautifully against his rich cocoa skin and the white turban-like wrap around his head lets me know there is an army of dreads dying to come out and flow down his shoulders which would make him heavenly all over again.

Our eyes meet and greet for a second time and my heart won't let me summon the courage to tell this stranger, as delicious as he is, that I love him dearly, already. He is divinity and purgatory all rolled into one masterful man of perfection. I want him.

He passes me by and I thank God I got the opportunity to see him once more.

After many drinks, a few rounds at the slot machines and one too many chocolate candies, the "itis" has kicked in and I excuse myself, leaving my girls to go get some rest. My body really needed this vacation. I arrive at my cabin. Taking off my shoes and my cream-colored halter sundress, I prepare to take a shower, but before doing so, I have the nerve of a glutton, and I order room service. A slice of chocolate cake and two scoops of chocolate ice cream with hot fudge deems appropriate since this is a vacation.

I love the way this ship has the shower gel and everything you need right here on the wall of the shower. How convenient. The water is steamy hot, just like I like it, and seems to awaken me just a bit, since I was a little sleepy just a while ago. I'm wide awake now. I'll soon be enjoying my chocolate cake and catching a good movie, putting my feet up and loving every minute of my personal paradise.

I dry off, put on my knee length aqua-colored silk robe and walk out of the bathroom. Perfect timing. There's a knock at the door.

How do I breathe again? Okay, I think I exhale, then inhale, okay, yes, that's it, inhale, okay, I got it. Calm down. Breathe. Nice and easy. It's gonna be alright. Ebony majesty greets me with a smile and pushes my cart into my room. I'm weak.

"Thank you, Sir," I say trying to sound sexy, polite and courteous.

He places the cart in the center of my cabin, between my bed and the dresser that sits below the television. Approaching me as he prepares to leave my room, I reach into my bag for tip money, when he stops me, grabs my hand, loosens the belt to my robe, places his hand gently on my right breast, runs his fingers down to my abdomen, and then pushes me back slightly onto the bed.

"Fuck my face and grab my dreads," he says to me while dropping to his knees, spreading my legs as far as they'll go. Wide, determined licks coat my sugar walls and he devours me with his tongue. Grabbing his dreads and pulling them, grinding on his face, I'm in the midst of pure ecstasy, and can't believe what I'm allowing to take place.

"Your pussy tastes so sweet," he tells me as he comes up just slightly for air. "Let me drink your nectar. Release all of your juice onto my lips."

His words alone take me there. I'm fucking his face so hard, slow and forceful moves from my hips pushes my pussy further into his face, and he loves it. He grabs my hips and sucks on my pussy, gently bites my clit which makes me cum instantly. Taking his two fingers, he fucks me with them while sucking my clit like a rabid dog.

Go, Cujo, I say to myself knowing that this shit is not real. I must be dreaming. If I don't stop yelling, somebody is going to call security, I'm sure of it.

The feeling becomes too intense for me, and I try to move from his face, but there's no use. He spreads my ass even further, reaching back to the tray, he takes a handful of chocolate ice cream, smears it all over my ass, onto my pussy, in my hole, it's so cold, and his lips—so hot.

Licking, kissing, sucking, smacking my ass, he eats the ice cream and me so well; he's fucking with me. He licks my asshole, sticking his tongue in it, bites my ass, sucks on my cheeks, fucks me with his tongue—damn, he's fucking with me even more. I can't wait to fuck him. Instead, after I cum for the third time, he gets up, grabs a napkin from the tray, and wipes his mouth.

"Thank you, Lisa," he says as he makes his way to the door. I lean up and say, "Wait. What's your name?"

He gently closes the door behind him.

ক ক ক ক ক

"Girl, what happened last night? Or should I say this morning?" Regina says while all up in my face, grinning from ear to ear while at this breakfast table.

I smile and say nothing.

Paula leans in. "Was it that Rasta?"

Again, silence. I ain't saying shit, because in all honesty, I'm still trippin'.

We decide to go to the beach in Jamaica today and I am so happy because I've never been, for one, and secondly, because I don't want to run into his beautiful black ass. I'm shot out, no lie, and I've never done anything like that before. I guess I'm embarrassed. And as weird as it sounds, I'm really digging him and I don't even know his name.

Have you ever loved somebody, secretly loved somebody, you didn't know? I love a man who doesn't know me.

Drinks on the beach in Jamaica with my two best friends is a gift from God. It's a blessing really. It also lets me know that I am working hard for something. Sometimes we get so caught up in the hustle and bustle of life, in this fast-paced, microwave society, that we don't take time to smell the roses or reward ourselves. I didn't for many years while attending law school, working, clerking and building my own practice. I bust my ass for years to pay student loans, and just to keep a roof over my head that I never took time to enjoy life. Well, my attitude has changed and I will treat myself a lot more often. This is paradise.

After the beach and hours of sightseeing, we head back to the ship and agree to enjoy a buffet tonight for dinner as opposed to a fancier, more formal setting. I'm down with that.

I shower, change, and meet the girls in the Garden room. There are so many stations of different types of food here. I don't know what I want, I can't decide. I think I'll try some Chinese tonight. Chicken and broccoli has always been a friend of mine and sounds really good right now. Paula and Regina decide on American and Italian, respectively.

As I stand in line, the sweet smell of someone divine, along with the voice I want to hear for the rest of my life, penetrates all my senses as he whispers in my ear. "Randy." I turn my head slightly to look up at his perfectly chiseled, gorgeous ebony-infused face, perfectly straight white teeth, and deep set dark brown, sensual eyes, all atop his six foot two inch frame of steel and say, "Randy?"

"Yes. You asked my name. My name is Randy, Lisa. How are you this evening?"

He is a divine multitude of sin.

I blush. I'm wet. I want him, right now. Is it too early to tell him that I love him?

"I'm good, Randy." I want to ask him so many questions. However, before I can ask what possessed him to eat the pussy of a stranger, so well, I might add, he interrupts me.

"Meet me in my cabin, F240, in half hour," he says and walks away.

I don't have to think twice. I'll be there.

I never did get the chance to eat. I was too anxious and nervous. I told the girls that I'd see them later. Went to my room and showered, fluffed my hair, baby-oiled my skin and headed to heaven, I mean F240.

The door is slightly ajar and I knock very lightly.

"Come in, Lisa."

"Hi, Randy." I see him sitting in the desk chair while sipping on what appears to be water with lemon.

Extending his hand, he motions for me to come over. "Come to me."

I walk over, not at all apprehensive, just comfortably, slightly nervous and elated. I straddle him and wrap my arms around his neck, peck him on his lips, kiss him softly, while he grabs my waist, kisses my neck, and whispers in my ear. "Ride me."

I lift the skirt to the dress I'm wearing, as he pulls out the most beautiful chocolate dick I've ever seen. He strokes it with his hand, and smiles at me.

"Turn around. I can't love you face to face, I'll ejaculate too quickly and I want to fuck you all night long."

I get up, still in awe over what just poured from his delicious lips. He has a way with words. I turn around and he pulls me toward him, removes my dress, and mounts me on his lap. I gently slide on his dick—it's so big, so rock hard, damn. As I slide down the shaft, I can tell he loves it as my pussy loves him, as he makes noises that make my clit throb with anticipation.

"You're so tight, baby. Let me love this sweet pussy real good for you." Grabbing my waist, lifting me up and down, my juices flow uncontrollably from my pussy, down to his balls, as I ride up and down this sweet pole. I reach around and look back at him, and he's feeling just as good as I am, and I know this. He places his head on my back, inhales deeply, kisses me, loves me.

"Damn, I want to love you for the rest of my life, Lisa. Can I have you baby?"

"I'm all yours Randy."

What the hell am I talking about?

Fuck it.

"Baby, please, don't lie to me. I want to be in this pussy for hours, Lisa. Please."

"Randy, this pussy is yours, baby."

"Your juicy pussy has my dick so wet from you releasing all over me. Damn, I love the way you feel. I need to have some more of you."

With that said he grabs my thighs, lifts me up and places me on my knees on his bed. Hitting me from behind, doggy style, causes us both to make noises that could awaken the dead.

"Bring that ass back to me, Lisa. Give it to me good baby."

I can't help myself. I match every one of his blows.

He pulls my hair, smacks my ass, and plunges into me so deeply. Damn, daddy long stroke is putting in work.

"I love you, Lisa."

"I love you too, Randy."

We're both nuts. But it's okay. Just for tonight.

"Can I cum on you?" Randy asks me as the passion becomes too much for him.

"Yes, cum all over me, Randy, please."

Randy pulls out, and comes so hard all over my ass while yelling in ecstasy.

❧ ❧ ❧ ❧ ❧

Waking up in Randy's arms is the highlight of my trip thus far. He has his arms around me as I lay on his chest, kiss his nipples softly.

"No, Lisa, I can't handle that right now, baby," he says to me as he moves in closer to my face. He rubs my cheek, caresses my face with his fingers. "You're so beautiful."

"Thank you, Randy. I have a question."

"Anything, Lisa. Ask me anything."

"Have you ever done this before?"

"Done what, sweetheart?"

"Done what we've just done. Make love to a stranger."

"No, I've never had a one-night stand on the cruise ships, Lisa. And to me, you're not a stranger. I feel like I've known you forever. This is a first for me."

I can say no more. I really don't know what to do other than rest in his arms.

"Do you want some breakfast, Lisa?"

"That depends on what breakfast is?" I say while licking his nipple once more.

"Ha ha. What do you have a taste for?" Randy asks me while bending down, putting my breast into his mouth, placing his hand onto my pussy.

"Well, Randy, I could go for something chocolate this morning."

I slide under the sheet and find my new best friend. I take my tongue and swirl it around the tip, slowly taking him into my mouth, he moans in ecstasy as I reach his balls and lick them too. I figure I'd return the favor, and down him so good. Giving him head this morning is a good enough breakfast for me. And by the sounds coming from his mouth, I think he's just satisfied with it.

"Damn, girl. You betta watch yourself. I just may fall in love with you over and over again," he says after I tantalize him with every inch of my tongue.

"Again?" I question.

"Yes, again, Lisa. I know it seems so stupid, and I am probably a fool for it, but I'm falling in love with you."

Silence.

❧ ❧ ❧ ❧ ❧

After six days and nights of lovemaking, the inevitable is upon us and we both realize this as we stand on the balcony outside of the main deck. From behind, Randy wraps his arms around me, leans in to my cheek and kisses it softly. I tell him, "I'm sure gonna miss you, baby."

Pulling me in closer to his magic, he whispers again softly in my ear, "I don't want this to end."

"It has to Randy. I live in Newark, New Jersey and you work on a cruise ship. There's no way this can go on. I wish I could spend the rest of my life with you, I do. But we both know what reality is."

I give Randy my number and address, knowing full well that this is indeed the end. He kisses me softly on my forehead and tells me, "I love you, Lisa."

"I love you more, Randy," I respond teary-eyed as he closes the door to our taxi.

I've never loved anyone the way I love Randy, never. I thank God for the time we shared, although I feel so empty inside. This week on the cruise proves to me that all men are not created equal. Just too bad I had to leave my life's dream in Miami.

❧ ❧ ❧ ❧ ❧

Back to the grind, it's been a full week since our cruise, since I saw Randy—smelled him, made love to him, allowing myself to fully receive the love of a good man. I miss him so much. As I pick up a fresh cut of salmon here at the grocery store, I smile because during one of our eat in dinners in my cabin, he ordered salmon; said it was one of his favorite meals. I plan to make it tonight.

My usual occurs, especially after such a long day of depositions, and two court appearances, I'm beat. I take a nice, long, hot shower, sip on white zinfandel, turn on a little jazz, and prepare my meal. Prepare Randy's salmon as if he were here. I pick up the phone to dial him, but hang up, I'm so stupid.

It was just a fling, Lisa…

Who the hell is ringing my damn doorbell this late?

I tighten my robe, look through my bay window curtains and see the silhouette of a man. Can't be. Naah. No way.

I crack the door open.

Remember that breathing thing again, Lisa. Inhale, exhale, slow, be easy.

"You thought I'd let you out of my life that easily?" Randy makes his way into my home, looking as delicious as he possibly can, roses in one arm, champagne in another.

I toss the roses and champagne onto the sofa, and then proceed to kiss my man with all the passion I can muster. Deep tongue kisses, heavy breathing, licking and sucking on every inch of him. He can't get a word in.

He laughs. "Lisa, baby. Can we talk?"

"Not right now, sweetheart." I pull him closer to me. "You know, I'm making your favorite dinner baby."

"Is that right?"

"Yes, it is. Well, depending on what you have a taste for, Randy."

"Grab my dreads and fuck my face, Lisa."

I oblige.

I pinch myself the morning after to make sure I'm not dreaming. Making love to Randy all night and waking up in his arms has to be a dream.

"What do we do now, Randy?" I kiss his nipples once again as I lay on his chest, finding comfort in his arms.

"I'm here now, baby. I want to be your everything, Lisa. Can we start there?"

Dubbed the "Queen of Hip Hop Romance Erotica" by *Disilgold Soul Magazine*, **ELISSA GABRIELLE** is the author of two poetry books, *Stand and Be Counted* and *Peace in the Storm*, and the highly-acclaimed novel *Good to the Last Drop,* and the sequel *Point of No Return* (August 2007), as well as the much anticipated novel *A Whisper to a Scream* (Christmas 2007). She is the founder of the greeting card line, Greetings from the Soul: The Elissa Gabrielle Collection. Gabrielle has graced the covers of *Conversations Magazine*, *Big Time Publishing Magazine*, and *Disilgold Soul Magazine*. Visit the author at www.elissagabrielle.com.

Rendezvous

Gabrielle Chaveau looked at her watch impatiently as she raised her other arm and imperiously snapped her fingers for an airport taxi. With her creamed honey complexion and hourglass figure, the cabbies were fighting each other to be the first to answer her call. The one who succeeded skidded to a stop and popped out of his car with a broad grin like he had just spiked a winning touchdown. She barely noticed as she absently directed him to put her Louis Vuitton luggage in the trunk, too engrossed in the conversation she was having on her cell phone to pay him much attention.

After she finished her conversation, she snapped her cell closed with a decisive flip of her hand.

"Where to, miss?"

"1224 Mystery Court."

"In Beau View Gardens?"

"Yes," she answered crisply. He gave a low whistle.

"High rent district up there. You need lots of ducats to live in that development." He looked expectantly in the rearview mirror after he had eased his way into the exiting airport traffic.

She ignored him, choosing instead to carefully lay her head back on the cracked and splitting vinyl and close her eyes. She found this to be a helpful and effective device to stop any unsolicited and unwanted conversation. The cabbie, realizing that she wanted no conversation, still could not resist stealing peeks at the beautiful woman in his cab.

Thanks to her African-Antiguan/Cuban mother with her warm, brown skin and her Irish/French-Canadian father with his piercing blue eyes, she had been graced with long, thick chestnut brown hair that flowed over her head and shoulders and ended in soft, bouncy curls that accentuated her startling blue eyes. She looked ethnically indefinable, and she liked it that way. It kept people guessing.

Unbeknownst to the cabbie, Gabrielle knew every time he snuck a peek at her. After a while, however, she completely closed her eyes as she let a soft smile gently play about her mouth. She was looking forward to this time away from the office and the craziness of life in the big city. The best thing about this place was the outstanding concierge service available. Catering services were only a phone call away. It was like being in a hotel while still having the privacy of your own home.

Now that all the desired changes were finally complete, she was looking forward to seeing the two-bedroom, two-bath sprawling ranch that was built in a U around a heated, azure pool with the disappearing edge that looked like it met the ocean beyond. Gabrielle thought it well worth the two-and-a-half-million-dollar price tag.

After reaching the house and unlocking the massive mahogany double doors, Gabrielle paid the still grinning cabbie, and then closed the door with a sigh of relief.

Glancing at her watch, she noted the time. After snatching up her bag, she raced to the master bedroom, stripping along the way. She stopped briefly in front of the mirror to analyze her figure. She sometimes worried that her breasts were too big or her hips too wide, but thank goodness she still had her flat stomach and small waist.

Realizing that time was of the essence, she picked up the cordless phone and succinctly placed a dinner order with specific instructions as to the preparation and time of arrival. That done, she moved into the floor-to-ceiling, peach-colored, Italian travertine marble bathroom, turning on the six heads, and quickly showered. After drying off, she anointed her body with Beyond Paradise lotion and a spritz of the same fragrance.

Perusing her lingerie, she decided on a skimpy, beige, lace-trimmed baby-doll negligee shot through with golden threads that floated over her body and set off her honey-toned skin to perfection. She donned the matching gold mules and opted to forego the thong. Lightly dusting her cheeks with a bronze blush and her lips with a pale golden lip-gloss, she then added a sweep of gold on her lids that brought out the flecks of gold in her blue eyes, and black mascara on her already indecently long eyelashes.

Glancing at her clock on the vanity, Gabbi smiled as she realized that her timing was perfect. Just at that moment, she heard a key scrap the lock in the door. She picked up a remote, hit play, and Dave Koz's seductive sax poured out of the hidden speakers.

Sauntering slowly and seductively toward the front door, she arrived there just as Daniel put down his own bag and turned around. The sight of Gabbi brought a grin to his lips and a tightening in his groin.

"Hey, baby. How was your flight?" she asked him before moving into his arms and throwing a lip lock on him before he had a chance to answer.

Daniel let his hands roam over Gabbi's back, his big hands clasping her firm, full ass, pulling her hard against him as he moved against her nether lips, which caused him to groan as he caressed her soft, fleshy ass. It was toned, but just full enough

171

to be squeezable, just how he liked it. It had been too long since he'd had her in his arms. Between his basketball schedule and her business schedule, as well as other obligations, getting a chance to meet at their house was getting to be next to impossible.

Jumping into Daniel's arms, Gabbi wrapped her legs around his waist as they continued to tongue each other down while he walked toward the wide, cocoa-colored, suede sofa sectional. Every time his magnificent hardness pushed against her, she wanted to feel it stroking deep inside her, she felt her valley clinch in anticipation and need.

Just looking at Daniel was enough to give even grandmothers erotic wet dreams. It didn't make any sense for one man to be that damn fine. Almost seven feet tall, black as an ace of spades, bald-headed with almond-shaped eyes the color of a panther's, and silky eyebrows completed his chiseled good looks. He was a Howard University graduate with a degree in business management, could hold a decent conversation, was surprisingly funny, refined, and smooth as a piece of Godiva chocolate. Gabbi found him totally irresistible even though she knew she shouldn't indulge her need for this particular piece of chocolate.

"Go take your shower. Dinner should be here any minute," Gabbi told him, slowing down their foreplay.

Daniel had just stepped into the shower when their food arrived. Gabbi had the attendants place the food on the serving cart out on their patio where hot pink and white trails of bougainvillea lazily swayed in the gentle breeze through the overhead pergola. She gasped and then giggled when she felt the still-damp Daniel grab her from behind and nuzzle her neck. Turning around, she sighed as she ran her hands over his muscled, bare chest, letting her fingers gently tease his already hard nipples. She glanced down and was pleased to see his hardness jump under the low-slung towel he wore.

"Keep that up and we'll never get to eat," she teased.

"I'm hungry, but it ain't for food," he told her in his deep voice that strummed like a cord though her being, causing a shiver to chase itself down her spine and settle between her legs. Pulling Gabbi to him, he plundered her mouth as he walked her backward across the patio while their tongues danced with one another. His hands palmed her ass as he picked her up, prompting her to wrap her legs around his waist.

They stopped when his legs hit the edge of the heavy, mosaic, stone table with the thick, wrought-iron base. Daniel gently released Gabbi, letting her slide down his body and dislodging the towel in the process. He finally released her soft, full lips, leaving a trail of hot kisses from the side of her face to her ear, to her neck, and down to her breasts that were almost popping out of the top of her gown.

"Dance with me," Gabbi softly demanded as she started to move her body seductively against his. The music had changed from Dave to Janet and she was feeling how love goes as she grinded and undulated against and around his body.

Daniel watched her through the slits of his eyes, his breath coming in shallow breaths, his hardness growing more painful with each sweep of her body against his.

"You want this?" she asked, mimicking the next song playing.

"Fuck, yeah," he answered, spurred on by her movements against his body. Not caring about the cost of the expensive dishes, or the food, he pushed it all off the table and put her on it after ripping off her flimsy gown.

"Now that's what I'm talking about," he murmured as he stopped for moment to gaze at her luscious figure. "Baby, you looking like a seven course meal to me. Your lips, mmmm," he said as he sucked them into his mouth and then forced his tongue inside—"are the appetizer. And you know how much I love me some neck-bones." He chuckled as he sucked on her neck, making her juices flow and causing her to strain against his mouth.

"Girl, and these luscious melons you call breasts are sweet as homemade wine," he said before teasing first one hard peak and then the other, paying homage to both of them. He pushed her voluptuous breasts together and went rapidly back and forth between them, sucking her nipples to the point of distraction, and then finally managing to suck them both into his mouth at once, causing Gabbi to cry out in need.

Gabbi was panting and could feel her wetness running down her thighs, her being craving to have Daniel's twelve inches stroking the places deep in her valley that only he could reach.

When he finally released her now-swollen breasts and nipples, he moved to her quivering stomach, kissing his way down and stopping briefly to dip and swirl his tongue in her belly button. Pulling up a chair, he sat down as her thighs gaped open, leaving her fully exposed to his ravenous gaze.

"Girl, now see, this is what I'm talking about. Love me some mussels with your special sauce," he murmured as he delicately pulled her nether lips apart, revealing her glistening pearl within. Gabbi was panting as she leaned up on her arms and watched Daniel as he leaned forward. When his tongue swept between her lips, she gasped and almost fell backward, but managed to keep herself up so she could watch as Daniel's large, pink tongue lapped her from her ass to her clit. Her legs were trembling as the sensations washed over her.

When he pulled her ass to edge of the table, she finally gave in and lay back on the table as her legs opened wider to accommodate the new position. Daniel quickly took advantage of the position and scooted his chair closer to the object of his desire. Inserting a finger into her hot, dripping valley, he slowly moved it in and out, feeling Gabbi grab and throb around his finger. He added another finger and felt her lift off the table as he watched her bud grow and swell, prompting him to capture it with his lips and gently suck it. Gabbi moaned loudly and began to rotate against his fingers in an effort to speed up her release. Daniel alternated between stroking her slowly and then fast, feeling her wetness run down his fingers as she clutched them with her muscles. The taste and smell of her was driving him almost insane. Just when he felt she was ready to explode on his fingers, he abruptly stood, lifting her with him while still sucking her clit. Then in one smooth move his hardness replaced his fingers, wrenching a scream of pleasure from Gabbi as she clutched him to her with her legs and let her overdue orgasm flow over Daniel's hardness.

Daniel, as much as he wanted to drive himself completely into Gabbi's tight wetness, knew that to do so might end up with her in the hospital. He gritted his teeth and slowed his movements, letting Gabbi do most of the thrusting, trusting that she would know how far to push up on him. But it was driving him mad not to indulge his need to totally sheath himself deep inside her. Had he not been quite as wide, it might have been possible, but being wide and long made it impossible. Still, the fact that she could handle a good nine inches was better than most.

Now as he felt the suck and release of her pussy walls on him, his balls tightened and his breath came in hard, shallow gasps. Sweat ran down his face and plopped on her stomach as he fought a battle to hold back. It had been so long. He felt himself losing the fight. Looking down, he marveled at how his member looked, all shiny with Gabbi's juices as it plunged in and out of her deep, pink heaven. It was erotic as hell to watch himself move in and out of her swollen pussy lips and to hear her beg him not to stop, to give it to her hard, to fucking *cum*.

Both were gasping for breath as they fought to bring the other to completion. Every time Gabbi raised up and let Daniel slip a little deeper inside, he felt himself getting ready to lose his mind from how good it felt. When he hit that spot that it seemed only he could reach, Gabbi squeezed her eyes closed and a low rumbling sound that escalated into a high pitch note turned into a mouth open, soundless scream as she climaxed so hard that she thought she was going to pass out.

When Gabbi climaxed like that, it felt like she had opened up from deep within and sucked almost all of Daniel inside of her, and then it was as if he was getting head from the *slurp-suck* that her walls did to him, making his toes curl and his eyes cross. He clutched her ass and hammered her pussy so fast and furiously that they both lost their breaths. He came so hard inside her that it made her insides dance and she joined him yet again in ecstasy. She felt tears slip out of her eyes and run down the sides of her face as they both cried out their completions in unison.

Slowly they floated back down to reality and Gabbi became aware of bits of food and dishes under her, along with Daniel's weight on top of her. Gently pushing him off, she sat up, looked around, and surveyed the mess.

"I guess we're going to have to order pizza again, huh?"

"Yeah, I guess." He chuckled ruefully as he stood, stretched, and helped her off the table.

Padding back into the house naked, she placed another order and was getting ready to jump into the shower when she heard Daniel's cell phone. Picking it up, she glanced at it, and then went back outside and handed it to him as it continued to ring.

"Here. It's Giselle."
"Your sister?"
"Yeah. And your wife."

GAYLE JACKSON SLOAN is a native of Philadelphia, but has lived in Akron, Ohio, Pittsburgh, and Washington, DC. Gayle has loved to read and write since she was four years old. Growing up, she used to write volumes and volumes of poetry that was inspired by the syncopated rhythms of Maya Angelo and the freestyle of Nikki Giovanni. Life, however, has a way of sometimes getting in the way and she put aside her poetry to raise her daughter. When she picked up *Disappearing Acts* by Terry McMillan, she said to herself, "I can do this!" Encouraged by her mother and husband, she started two books that were still languishing in the bottom of a drawer. However, it wasn't until the passing of her beloved mother that she finally finished her first novel, *Saturday's Child*, which she first self-published.

Amid personal tragedies, upheavals, and general chaos, she struggled tenaciously to finish her second novel, Wednesday's Woes , which is a follow up—not a sequel—to her first novel. She attended Philadelphia University where she studied interior design. She is currently a legal assistant at a prestigious law firm. When she is not writing, reading or gardening, she is teaching her grandchildren to say "Nana is a Diva!"

She is currently working on her third and fourth novels, *Dancin' In My Shoes* and *Let the Necessary Occur*.

Babygirl Blue

I couldn't believe it had been three-hundred-sixty-five days since Trey walked out on me. I hated to think about him or our relationship because it reminded me so much of my emptiness. Thinking about him took me back to the day he broke my heart in two.

At the time, Trey had been my live-in beau for two years. He meant the world to me and no one could have told me that one day I, Sasha Jordan, was not going to be his wife. I would not have believed them. I would have called them a liar and told them the truth wasn't in them. Then I would have cursed them out on sheer principal.

The only wedge we had between us was his pesky baby mamma and her drama, but I was confident the love Trey and I had for one another could overcome any mess Sanquetta pitched our way. Boy was I wrong! When Trey chose to make a life with her and their daughter it came only minutes after he professed his undying love for me. First, he made love to my body and mind. I was floating in the clouds and could have lived there for weeks, but I came crashing down when he left out my door never to return again.

My world had not been the same since then. As much as I hated it, the man still had a permanent residence in my heart and so far, I had been unsuccessful in evicting him. Against my better judgment, I allowed my mind to travel back to the day that I often played over again down to the last second. The day he left.

On this particular day, I walked through my foyer after a long day at work to find Trey sitting on the sofa watching an X-rated movie. He usually worked third shift, so I was surprised to find him awake, much less sitting in the living room with a hard-on watching porn. I rolled my eyes and walked in the opposite direction of him without speaking. Those movies turned him into a horn dog and I knew before I could get my foot in the door good he would be ready to relieve some of that frustration on me and I wasn't in the mood. After the drama filled day I had, all I wanted to do was blend up a strawberry daiquiri and lay down with a good book.

"Hey babe!" Trey jumped at the sound of the door closing behind me and pressed the stop button on the DVD player. He must have noticed my sour mood because he asked attentively, "How was your day Sasha?"

I looked over my shoulder to see he was practically on my heels.

"Like every other day in that hell hole Trey. What makes today any different?" I put my keys on the key holder and proceeded into the kitchen. I worked as a financial advisor for Gold Financial and between irritating customers and my co-workers, I was going to hurt somebody one day.

I continued, "Kenzie did everything she could to dodge work leaving everything on me as usual, that woman knows how to get on my last nerve. Just wait until I tell you what the heifer had the nerve to say to me today." He stood and listened as I spit out what was on my mind. Something he was used to.

Kenzie was my lazy co-worker who always kept some office chaos brewing. She did as little work as possible yet always managed to make the monthly bonus that I pulled the weight for. Today her clown performance included getting into my personal business. I overheard her telling Linda that Trey had been seeing Sanquetta behind my back. That lying heifer didn't know what my man was doing. Just last week she told me that Linda's husband was cheating on her, so what gives?

I plopped my briefcase down on the kitchen table, washed my hands in the sink, plugged in the blender and took out some strawberries and gin. Out the corner of my eye, I could see Trey's sexy abs glistening like he had just showered and rubbed lotion on his body. Trey was the only man I knew that took time out to lotion his entire body down including his feet every time he took a shower and I loved that about him. His confident swagger, bare muscular chest and the hypnotizing bulge through his boxers did not go unnoticed either.

Trey was the first dark-skinned man I dated and we had been hot and heavy since the day we met. Boy, I didn't know what I was missing. Not that his complexion was a major factor. When I have love for someone, I love them hard and deep no matter what. However, it never ceased to fail when I saw Trey's dark, chocolate barely naked body I wanted to eat him up. He was 217 pounds 6 feet 3 inches of pure eye candy.

As I stood over the sink preparing my relaxing potion, I felt his warm hands gently massage my shoulders, his hard body pressed snuggly against my rear. The command he had over me, relieved more tension than any session I'd had with my therapist. It was as if he made all of my problems disappear with the stroke of his hand. I was mentally zonked from my long day at work, so I still had my attention focused on blending up the daiquiri and finishing up *Defining Moments* by Jacquelin Thomas; however, I closed my eyes, took a deep breath and enjoyed the massage my man was graciously giving me.

Then out of nowhere Babygirl made her presence known, she was a force to be reckoned with too. I knew there would be no sense in trying to fight her. She had a whole different game plan and ninety-nine percent of the time, she got her way. The heat from Trey's touch had her pulsating and creaming inside my panties. You see, Babygirl is the nickname Trey coined for my pussy the first time he explored her. She had him moaning and screaming, "Ooooo baby—girl!!" this and "Ahhh…baby girl!!" that all night long. That night she got her name and took on a life of her own.

"What did she say?" Trey's hot breath barely above a whisper in my ear pulled me from deep inside my pleasures.

What did she say? I couldn't remember anything but my name at that moment. His body heat up against mine warmed me to the core. Before I could part my lips to attempt to formulate an answer, he raised my skirt exposing my pink thong and softly nibbled on my ear. His lips felt heavenly against my skin. He gingerly moved his powerful hands to my plump behind caressing each cheek.

I somehow managed to swallow the lump in my throat and said, "We…we…we can talk about it later."

My issues with Kenzie could wait. There was no way I was going to discuss her with Trey while he was standing at attention. If I could help it, I would be the only woman on his mind in those moments.

Trey got the hint and ceased all conversation, he let his trail of kisses from my neck down my back do the talking for him all while working his fingers over Babygirl's swollen lips. He rubbed my clit with just the right amount of pressure to beam me up into utopia massaging the material over my breasts with his free hand. That's what I liked about Trey, he knew what I wanted and perfected it every time. He knew that gentle finger action before sex drove me wild. Don't get me wrong; I like it rough as much as the next woman but a gentle tease first made it all the sweeter. Plus, he knew he couldn't just ram his colossal stick inside me without some foreplay. Uh...uh...Babygirl wasn't made for that.

I surrendered to his soothing assault and leaned the back of my head back into his chest grinding Babygirl up against his juicy fingers. His gigantic hands were one of the attractions that drew me to him. I love a man with big hands.

"Mmmmmm." I moaned as he stroked Babygirl's bud the way she loved him to until my body trembled and she released a river of love juices. My eyes rolled to the back of my head and I felt my legs getting weak, so I clinched the kitchen sink to brace myself.

Hell to the yeah! Ain't nothing like coming home from a stressful day at work to a man who specializes in de-stressing the booty...Okay! I thought. When it came to putting in work, Trey got Employee of the Month in this mutha!

He licked his lips and damn near smacked the juices off of them. "You taste so good Sasha," Trey said and I could feel my body tremble to the notes in his baritone voice.

"Take me now Trey!" I exhaled, my voice heavy with desperation. It was amazing how fast the tables turned on me. When I walked through the door I didn't want to be bothered with him and twenty minutes later I'm practically begging for penetration. That's the kind of power he had over Babygirl. I was strong enough to resist, but Babygirl was weak.

"Slow your roll," he said, "I see I wasn't the only one with a lot of pent up frustration today, so don't get to trembling on me yet Sasha, the party has yet to begin." Trey smiled showing his intoxicating grin.

Was there anything about him that didn't turn me on?

"Whatever," I said, unsuccessfully trying to sound blasé, all the while knowing Trey was about to rock my world just like he did every other time we made love.

At least he could back up every word of his trash talking. He was not a two-inch brother bragging about toting a python. He had the total package: the magic stick, tongue action, finger action, and don't be fooled, his left stroke was the death stroke. I was starting to see why some women paid for the magic stick. Let's face it. He had me on sprung.

He spun me around to face him and kissed me passionately. He tugged slightly on my bottom lip as he deepened the kiss after kissing for what seemed like an eternity only breaking the kiss to boast.

"You know I'm the first and last brotha who knows what to do with Babygirl. I can make Babygirl cum without even touching her."

He flashed his charismatic grin and confirmed his last statement. His handsome face and gorgeous grin sparked another pool of wetness to flow down my legs without him even touching me. I unbuttoned my skirt and stepped out of it. I stripped out of the rest of my clothes with the quickness.

I couldn't take it any longer, I pointed toward the bedroom, and "Trey Babygirl can't take this. She wants you inside now!"

The journey to my bedroom was a long one, but I wouldn't have had it any other way. Trey left his boxers on the kitchen floor, picked me up into his arms and made way to the bedroom. In the hallway, he stopped, pinned me against the wall and sucked my neck hungrily, he kissed my lips with the same fever caressing my tongue with his. The deep moans that escaped from his throat made my heart melt. I felt my lower body was about to explode. He licked a trail from my chin down to Babygirl while he held my body steady against the wall. My eyes fixed on his baldhead as he moved his tongue back and forth assaulting Babygirl until I felt like I was going to pass out from pleasure. Forget a daiquiri I was drunk off his loving.

"I'm about to cum Trey. Make me cum baby." I screamed as my orgasmic washed over my petite brown frame.

Three hours later and after a brief nap, I lay in the bed entangled in the covers next to Trey. I turned over under the covers to look at him; I could not get enough of my Chocolate King. He was all a woman could ask, need or desire in and out of the sheets. It was days like these that made me realize why I surrendered my heart to him in the first place. I counted my blessings that I was able to come home to him every day and lay down with him every night.

The porn industry was worth its weight in gold, I thought. Trey tried every position possible on me. The frog leap and deep stick positions were my favorite. We climaxed during the frog leap twice.

I nestled up close to him until I felt safe in his muscular embrace. His massive body completely covered me and I fit perfectly into his grooves as if we were made for each other. I would have spent the rest of my life just like that if I could. It didn't take long before he stirred from his slumber and expanded to his full length giving me the go ahead to get round two underway. I straddled him and just when I felt my passion ignite the phone rang.

The caller ID showed it was Trey's daughter's mother, Sanquetta, calling from her cell phone so we decided to let her call go to the answering machine. After the beep her irritating voice rang out, "Trey, this is San. It's urgent that I talk to you. Call me as soon as you get this message."

Everything was urgent to Sanquetta, which was nothing new. According to her, all of her calls were important. Even when she called begging for sex.

Trey pulled me close to him and said, "I talked to Cherise right before you got home from work today and everything was fine. I'll call her back in a little while babe, now where were we."

I straddled him again when the phone rang for the second time. After her fourth call in eight minutes, I picked up the phone before Trey could. Sanquetta was a bugaboo but she had never called back to back like that.

"I'll get it Trey. You know she doesn't like to talk to me, so if it's not important it won't take long."

"Hello?" Trey ran his finger up and down my back as I talked.

"Hello Sasha. Put Trey on the phone," Sanquetta was blunt.

I let out a sound of disgust. "Trey is sleeping. What do you need?" Note I said "need" because as far as I was concerned she definitely wasn't getting what she wanted, my man.

"Look Sasha, put him on the phone it's important." I was two seconds away from hanging up the phone but I wanted to make sure nothing was wrong with my stepdaughter. "Is Cherise okay?"

Sanquetta knew I was not going to give Trey the phone unless she had a valid reason for her call, so she spit it out. "No Sasha, she's not. She's been admitted to the hospital and she has been asking for her daddy for over an hour. Trey needs to come to Shady Memorial Hospital right away. "

I could tell from the alarm in her voice that she was being truthful. She had never lied about Cherise's safety.

"Oh, my God! What's the matter? Is it her asthma?"

"Yes, and it's really bad! So would you please just let me speak to Trey?"

I handed Trey the phone without further interrogation.

Needless to say, he quickly dressed and left for the hospital. He didn't want to take me along for fear that Sanquetta and I would end up fighting it out over Cherise's hospital bed.

I would never do anything like that and I told him as much, but I didn't argue with him. It was more important for him to be there for his daughter than to be at home arguing with me, so I let it go. I kissed him goodbye and he has never walked through my door again.

When he finally answered his cell phone a week later, he explained that seeing Cherise in the hospital, with all of the tubes hooked up to her, made him realize how fast he could lose her. He wanted to be able to be with her everyday and watch her grow up. Kiss her knee when she fell and scraped it and help her with her homework. He wanted to be there for her when she was sick, and not have to be tracked down.

There was nothing I could say or do to convince Trey that we were meant for each other and that he could do all of those things with me as his wife. His mind was made up and his resolve solid. When I hung up the phone, I fell onto my bed and poured my heart into my pillow.

What started out a nice trip down memory lane was interrupted by the harsh reality. Trey was gone, for good. I had to come to grips that Jack Daniels was not going to mend my broken heart, and neither was my dildo able to satisfy my sexual desires. With a year of celibacy under my belt Babygirl was begging for a comeback.

Stop whimpering around over some lost inches, Babygirl chastised me. *It's not like he's the only man in town packing. Get up, get dressed and let's go get our groove back tonight,* Babygirl was officially off hiatus and taking charge. It was Saturday night, a perfect night for a one-night stand from the local nightclub.

I intuitively went into my walk-in closet and selected a form-fitting black dress and my diamond studded black stilettos.

"We can get sexier than that. Wear the pussycat suit and let the men see what I'm working with," Babygirl hyped me up to wear my skintight cat suit that I have not sported in years. *"I've waited a year for you to stop mourning Trey and move on to something bigger and better. Tonight, I'm officially getting back in the game.*

"Remember how I used to tremble when I was at the epitome of pleasure. Remember wave after orgasmic wave with a fine specimen to share it with. Remember that Sasha? I want that tonight. No, I need that tonight."

No matter what I did, I could not quiet Babygirl's voice. I also knew with her in this state there was no way I could quench her hunger mechanically.

One hour later, I was dressed in my black cat suit and diamond-studded black stilettos, and standing in front of Pleasure Castle, a dual women and men's strip club. Often times, couples came to Pleasure Castle to get roused up enough to go home and fulfill their mind blowing sexual fantasies. If I were lucky, I would find a soldier built to ride up in here.

Once I paid my twenty-dollar door charge and entered the club, a tall and ripped white guy approached me with a tray of drinks. "Welcome to Pleasure Castle where your wish is my command. Would you like a cocktail? The house drink is free all night."

Knowing everything that's free ain't good for you, I wondered what exactly was in the house drink mixture, but Babygirl could care less about the ingredients of the drink.

"Yes, we'll take the cock and you can have the tail," she blurted out, but from the look on the host's face, she spoke aloud.

"I think I can do that for you," the sexy host said as he took my hand and spun me around inspecting every inch of my skintight outfit. "I know a good thing when I see it." His skin was tanned to perfection. His topless body was pristine and baby oil covered muscles flexed in my face as he spoke.

"Fuck him!" Babygirl commanded me.

I quickly took the drink and almost tripped over someone trying to flee the Pleasure Castle worker. If I didn't find another delicious treat, I would get with him later but I wasn't just going to give it up to the first man that offered me a drink, and a free drink at that.

I pushed through the first crowd where men and a few lesbians were posted up gawking at the women strippers.

When I made it to the second stage I was elated. "Yes! I made it just in time for King Zulu!" King Zulu was the most well endowed stripper in all of the south. Try fifteen inches strong, no fillers or enhancers, just straight up dick. He was ripped in all the right places and had a baldhead just like I like them. Just fine.

I managed to get a center stage seat somewhere in the middle of the crowd and quickly rummaged through my purse to find the thirty singles I got from the gas station. I made sure I had enough change to work these strippers. I was about to tip Mandingo swinging King Zula at least half the money, if not all of it off the top.

As soon as I found the money, I started swinging it back and forth like I was losing my mind. Within minutes, he worked his way over to me.

"Lawd. Here he comes."

Touch it - bring it - pay it - watch it -turn it - leave it - stop - format it."

King Zulu swung his massive manhood around from woman to woman as he jammed to Busta Rhymes' Touch It beat. When he reached me, I took half the money in my hand and thrust it down into his Wonder thong screaming and panting like he was a superstar. I massaged the full length of his stick before reluctantly letting go.

Before I knew anything, King Zulu had me by the hand and up on the stage. My attempt at resistance was futile as he had ten times the strength in his powerful arms than I had in my entire body. Not to mention, his huge hand must have covered my entire upper arm.

"Come here babe. Don't be scared," he said in my ear with my legs now wrapped around his waist. "Let's give them a show."

"Please put me back in my seat." I managed to push through my lips.

Are you crazy? Babygirl said, "*Can we have our own private show later,*" she took over the conversation.

"Anything for you," King Zulu said.

Onstage, King Zulu grinded up against me in every position imaginable. I must have come at least three times just from the body contact. If what he did to me on the stage was a preview of what he had to offer in the bedroom, damn! His final act was to lay me down on the floor of the stage and stroke his manhood against my face. Before letting me go back to my seat, he placed a fat hickey on my neck and asked me to meet him backstage. He collected the remaining dollar bills from the stage floor and exited the stage.

Like a lovesick puppy (or even worse a groupie) within fifteen minutes I was standing at King Zulu's dressing room. I had freshened up as best as I could with the toiletries I had in my purse. When he opened his door, I looked up to see the tallest, darkest, finest man I had ever seen in my life. I was hypnotized by the look in his eyes. His aura was so familiar I had to be dreaming. His stage presence did not do justice to the real man up close and personal.

Instead of a formal greeting, he picked me up off my feet and kissed me long and deep on the lips. He carried me over to his plush sofa, sat me down gently like a piece of fine china and then returned to the door to lock it.

"I...I..." I began to explain that it was not everyday that I ran backstage with a stripper. As well, I wanted to know did he bring a different woman back stage every night he performed.

He placed a finger over my lips as if he predicted my ambivalence.

"First time for everything." He took three steps back from the couch and methodically performed a strip tease for me.

He removed the black and gray Wonder thong, the only piece of clothing he had left from his performance. When the thong hit the floor, I knew I was in trouble. I had bit off more than I could chew, even on a good day.

"Um...I think I better...um get going. This wasn't a good idea." I snuggled my purse up against my side closely. To hell if I was about to let him stick even half of that up in my tight puss. I wasn't trying to be up in the ER tonight with a repositioned uterus

"Don't worry. I'll be gentle." He stood in front of me with his manhood directly in my face. "Touch Blue he won't hurt you."

"Blue? Is that what you call him?"

"Yes." He stroked his hard flesh.

"Why do you call him that? I would think his name would be The Big Dipper or something like that."

He chuckled. "Well because most of the time I end up with blue balls when women get me roused up and then run away once they see what I'm working with.

"Well hell. We ain't running!" Babygirl let that be known with the quickness. *"Woman up Sasha! We going to end this drought with a big bang and King Zulu got dick for days, so what you waiting on?"*

I stood up and took over stroking Blue. "Well Mr. Blue, meet Babygirl." I removed my straps from my cat suit and wiggled out of it. I was glad Babygirl chose this outfit since I never wore underwear with it.

My perfectly shaven kitten purred as King Zulu dropped to his knees and began to devour me. He positioned one leg up on the couch and his hot tongue penetrated my skin unlocking desires that I never knew I had. With every stroke of his tongue another wave of pleasure came over me until his face was covered with my love juices.

When the tongue became more than I could handle, my legs buckled and I fell onto the softness of couch. I never received oral that damn near put me to sleep, but I was about to catch some Z's when King Zulu placed my legs over his shoulders and took my breasts into his mouth one at a time.

I opened my eyes and admired the fine specimen that mounted me. Then I remembered what he was working with and thought of ways I could squirm my way out of this compromising position.

"You will enjoy it. I'll be gentle." He must have read my facial expression. I wanted this man in the worst way, but I had doubts about taking on 15 inches my first time after a year of celibacy.

He retrieved a Magnum XXL off his table, applied it and rubbed some KY jelly onto the condom. *Thank God for that.*

I was sure going to need the extra lubricant. He reclaimed his place on top of me and kissed me gently like an old lover. Slowly, he slid inside me stroking with the tip at first easing in deeper inch by inch until he found a rhythm that was made for us. He traveled deeper and deeper with each stroke until he could not go any further.

"Oh…Zulu…Fuck!" I cried out.

He smothered my screams with more kisses. I tried to match his thrusts with my own once I got comfortable with the 11 or so inches I was receiving, but between his stick and body weight on top of me I was pinned in place. All I could do is tongue kiss my treat from Pleasure Castle and receive all that he had to offer me for tonight.

"You feel so good Sasha."

"You too…" Wait a minute…I didn't tell him my name.

He stood up taking me with him, never leaving my inner core, and sat down on the sofa with me in position to ride. I practically had to stand up to stroke his full length. At first, it hurt but with his coaching and gentleness pleasure overtook the pain and I came continuously like a leaky faucet. He massaged Babygirl heightening my pleasure beyond belief.

I knew he was about to cum when he quickened his pace and called out my name. "Oh right there Sasha. Keep it right there! Damn you feel so good girl."

I put every muscle in my back to work giving him the most sensual ride of his life. If I never saw him again after tonight he would remember me for a long time. We climaxed together and collapsed onto the couch.

Minutes later, I lay on his chest and after our breaths return to normal I asked, "How do you know my name?"

"So you really don't remember me, huh?" The puzzled look on my face told him I didn't, so he continued, "tenth grade. Mr. Calhoun's class."

His big black eyes and thick eyebrows jarred my memory and now I was taken aback. "Marlon Jackson? Oh my God, I had the biggest crush on you."

"Not as big as the one I had on you."

"My have you grown. I mean really *grown* into a fine man. I can't believe we just…"

"Yes, I just made love to you Sasha. I knew exactly what I wanted to do when I spotted you in the crowd." He tugged my chin so that our eyes met and I gave him my undivided attention. "I did what I've been wanting to since I first laid eyes on you years ago and you have not changed one bit. Just to see your pretty face, I've been banking at Gold Financial for the past year."

I knew my cheeks had to be flush red. I touched my hair nervously and said, "I can't believe this is happening to me." I didn't know what else to say. My body was on a sexual high and the first seed of love was planted in my heart at that very moment. His revelations made my body burn with more desire than I had when I first came backstage to meet him. We made love until sunrise and he put it on me so good that it was at least two weeks before I could walk straight.

As far as Blue goes…Babygirl will make sure Marlon won't be getting blue balls any time soon. King Zulu still performs at Pleasure Castle Thursday through Saturday, but now I have front row seats and a permanent backstage pass, just a few perks of being Mrs. Jackson.

What were the odds that Babygirl would talk me into a night of fulfilling her lustful desires and I would find something real in the process?

SHANI GREENE-DOWDELL lives in Opelika, Alabama with her three beautiful children and husband. She has always been fascinated by creative writing and, while reading interesting articles and book descriptions in ESSENCE magazine, she always told herself, "one day." Her day-to-day chores of motherhood had a way of taking her away from doing what she enjoyed most—expressing herself through paper and pen.

In 2005, with her children older, and her life more focused, she picked up her pen and started writing and hasn't put it down since. Whether she's writing poetry, blogging, writing book reviews for Big Time Publishing Magazine or working on one of her several upcoming projects, she is determined to follow her heart and become a best-selling author.

Her racy debut novel, *Keepin' It Tight*, was released May 2007. Shani is working on her sophomore novel, *Secrets of a Kept Woman*. For more information visit http://www.shanibooks.com or www.myspace.com/shanibouttoblowup.

Matrimonial Bliss

by Jessica Tilles
Author of *In My Sisters' Corner*

Chapter 1

On one knee, Samuel knelt down beside the bed and admired her elegant, yet strong, bone structure. In his eyes, she was perfection from her perfectly sculpted nose, to her pouty lips, to her deep, rich cocoa complexion. Fighting the urge to roll his finger over her curvaceous, regal figure lying beneath the satin sheet, her fine hips and shapely thighs had caused him to rise. Convinced she was all he needed, it was time to find out whether or not if the feeling was mutual. He had to find out now, before he acted on his rising nature, even though just hours before was a heated night of passion that smoldered every burning ember of her being.

With his eyes affixed on her beauty, Sam slowly, yet gently, making sure not to wake her, reached down and retrieved a dozen of freshly cut red roses he had hidden beneath the bed prior to the onset of their lovemaking. He closed his eyes and, to himself, silently whispered, "I love you more than you will ever know," before placing the heavenly scented bouquet on the pillow beside her face. This was a special occasion and it was only befitting for his Queen to wake up smelling roses.

Once again, he reached beneath the bed and retrieved a small Tiffany blue velvet box. Small enough for a ring, yet large enough for a pendant, and placed it on the pillow, beside the bouquet of roses.

She inhaled and sighed deeply, twitching around a bit. Then she inhaled again, the fresh rose scent aroused her from her slumber, and she slowly opened her eyes to the man who had made the last three years of her life the most loving she had ever experienced.

"Good morning." Free smiled widely, as she stretched her long voluptuous limbs around beneath the covers, loosening muscles that had stiffen from sleeping in her favorite position, spooned by the man who takes her breath away with his presence. Although the curtains were drawn, she rubbed her eyes as if she had awakened to the bright morning rays, as Sam looked on in awe. As she stretched her arms above her head, she pricked her arm on a single rose thorn. "Ouch!" Grabbing at her forearm, she gently rubbed away the sting of the minor prick. Then she rose up on her elbows, adjusted her eyes and stared down at the roses and tiny box that was strategically placed on her pillow, as she continued massaging her forearm. "What's this, honey?"

"Good morning, my Queen. I trust you slept well. You snored like you wouldn't believe," he chuckled.

"Hush, I don't snore." She hesitated, thinking on his comment for a quick second. "Did I really snore?"

Sam nodded and smiled.

Embarrassment blushed across her face. "Loudly?"

Sam nodded once again, but this time he smiled a smile of contentment that he had made the right decision.

"Why didn't you wake me?"

"Are you kidding me? I needed the rest."

"And," she said, pulling herself upright and leaning against the headboard. "What is *that* supposed to mean?"

"Never mind that for now." He nodded toward the bevy of red on her pillow. "How do you like your roses?"

"They smell wonderful, but I can't imagine where you got them. They surely don't look like roses from Free's Floral Boutique."

"Beautiful, sexy and brains to boot. A definite winning combination you are."

Free smiled at her ignorance. "The roses wouldn't have been a surprise had you gotten them from my boutique. Right?"

"Why Sherlock," he said, falling out with laughter. "I think she's got it!"

Free shook her head at his early morning silliness. She leaned over and felt the tiny box beneath her arm. "Ooh, what is. . ." Her mouth fell open as she realized, mid-sentence, what could be in the tiny box. "Samuel! Oh my God, honey!"

Sam too her hand in his and caressed it gently. "Sweetness, do you remember our very first date?"

Free's head lazily fell back against the headboard. Memories of the most embarrassing night of her life flooded her mind like an ocean's high wave crashing against the shores of Hawaii. "How could I forget it," she chuckled bashfully. And, even though their first date was three years ago, the thought of it remained with her and still made her queasy. "I was never so embarrassed in all my life. I knew I should not have eaten so much crab, but *no*, I had to go against what I knew was wrong and released myself up and down the road. I still have nightmares about Port-O-Pottys." She shook her head and released a hearty chuckle. "No, I'll *never* forget our first date, honey. Thanks for bringing it up."

Sam lowered his head and smiled to himself. Despite Free's mishap with the public toilets, when he first heard the sound of her sweet voice, she had given him butterflies. After a year of bachelorhood, Sam had given up on the idea of finding his soul mate. Actually, he was adamant one was nonexistent, until he laid eyes on Free, a bevy of chocolate decadence.

Sam took her hand in his and held it close to his lips, before placing the most delicate of kisses on each of her fingertips.

Chills shot through Free as she fought to restrain the urge building between her luscious thighs.

"Baby, do you remember what I said to you on our first date?"

Now she was becoming antsy. If he was going to pop the question, she wished he'd get it over with. She was dying to open the tiny box. She knew it was a ring. It was too small for anything else. "You said a lot of things, Sam." Her tone was annoying and rushed; he recognized it quickly.

Sam reached across her chest for the tiny box and kissed her on the cheek.

Free shot straight up in the bed and darted to the bathroom, knocking the bouquet of roses to the floor.

"Woman!" Sam shouted, picking up the bouquet and placing it back on the bed. "What are you doing?"

"I'm brushing my teeth."

"Couldn't that have waited?"

"It won't take long," she mumbled with a mouth full of Crest.

He heard her take in water, gargle, and spit into the sink. He cringed. Seeing someone brush their teeth was the ultimate turn-off. He closed his ears to her teeth brushing and concentrated on how he was going to pop the question. *Free, will you please do me the honor of being my wife? Nope, that's too corny. Baby, you are the best thing that has ever happened to me. I don't know what I'd do without you. Oh geesh, Sam, you can do better than that. Free Howard, make me the happiest man on God's green earth. Free, I love you, babe, and...*

His thoughts were interrupted as Free exited the bathroom, gleefully skipping toward the bed.

She knows, he thought. *Damn!*

Free grabbed her roses, smelled them and slipped under the covers. She smiled widely at Sam, like a child on Christmas morning.

Slowly Sam sat on the edge of the bed and pressed his palms against his thighs. He lowered his head, closed his eyes and said a prayer. He would not be able to stomach the embarrassment if she declined his proposal, even though deep down in his gut, he knew Free loved him more than anything but he never left anything to chance, nor took anything for granted, especially his woman.

Free was getting antsier by the second. She snatched up the box, placed it in the palm of her hand and extended it toward him. "Here, hurry up before I change my mind," she smiled. She knew Sam all too well and he wasn't the best at this kind of thing. He needed a slight nudge, and nudged him she did. "Come on, man!"

Sam chuckled as he rubbed his baldhead. "So, is that a yes?"

"Yes to what?"

Sam laid his hand on Free's covered knee. "Woman, I love you. It's been three of the best years of my life, ain't gettin' any younger—"

"No long speech, just get to the point," she giggled.

"Nothing would make me happier, Free—"

"Are you sure?"

A look of concern washed over his hazelnut complexion. "Do you have doubts?"

She took his face in the palms of her hand. "None, what so ever, my sweet, sweet baby."

"I love you, woman. More than you will ever know. I can't imagine…no, I don't want to imagine my life without."

The smile in her eyes contained joy and excitement for their future. "I know you do. I love you more."

Cupping her face, Sam's lips met hers. The softness of his lips pressed against hers sent chills throughout her being, and down between her thighs. She could hear the internal rumbling of an orgasmic explosion coming on.

Wrapping her arms around his neck, she pulled him into her and slowly reclined back onto the bed. She cooed as their tongues frolicked.

His hands roamed over her shoulder, down her arm and across her breast, firmly cupping it, causing her to loose her breath.

Her pants were quick and heated, her chest heaving as he firmly caressed the fullness of her breast.

As their lips parted, his tongue formed a wet, warm sensuous trail from her bottom lip, down and around her neck, where he gently nibbled, down to her breastbone, under each breast, continuing its trails over her belly, down toward her love.

As if on command, her legs parted instantly, allowing him access. With her hands affixed to the top of his smoothly shaven baldhead, she guided him toward the swelling protruding from the pink fleshy mound of sweet heavenly love.

He parted her Brazilian-waxed full lips, exposing the tiny knot he planned to enlarge as he gently stroked it. Each stroke as gentle as a feather and as intoxicating as the night before.

She flinched and her breath caught in her throat, as his tongue connected with her swollen clitoris. She stretched her arms above her head, plastering her palms flat against the headboard. The swivel of her hips intensified the desire she felt deep inside. It was a feeling she'd never felt before. . . until she met Sam.

"Hssss. Oooh, baby, that feels *so* good," she cooed, as she wrapped one leg around his neck. "Ohhhh, Daddy . . . ohhhh... yes, baby, yes–" she gasped for air as waves of pleasure consumed her being, sending electrifying chills up and down her spine, connecting with the deep arch in her back, as he raised the fleshy hood and concentrated on the tip of her swollen knot, driving her beyond crazy and into a whirlwind of euphoric uncontainable pleasure.

Free's hips swiveled and gyrated against his face. Wildly, she crossed her legs at the ankles and wrapped her legs snuggly around his neck, as she fucked his face, her clitoris rubbing with quick strokes against his mustache.

"Yes!" she yelled, grabbing the sheet and balling it into her fist. "Don't stop...baby. Right...there...don't...you...stop..." As if struck by a jolt of lightning, her legs flew open wide and trembled uncontrollably, as Sam held on tight for the ride. "Yes! Yes! *Yes*! *Oh*, yes!"

Sam feasted on the hot lava oozing from the opening of her cave.

"For the rest of our lives," she panted.

Sam nodded his head, his face still buried between her mounds of moist sex. "Until death do us part."

Crawling up from between her hot thighs, kissing them and moving up toward her abdomen, where he planted delicious kisses, he rested on the plumpness of her breast.

Free wrapped her arms around his shoulder and kissed the top of his head. "Samuel?"

"Um huh."

"Are you sure you want to marry me?"

He looked up at her. "I've never been surer of anything in my life. What about you?"

"I never block a blessing from God."

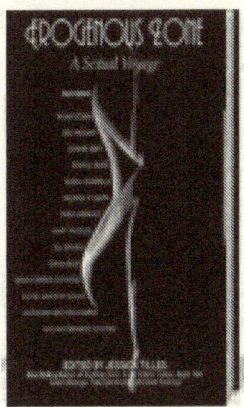

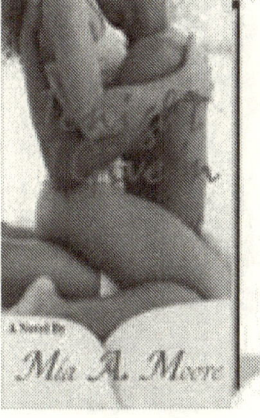

Fiction with Attitude...

www.xpressyourselfpublishing.org

Paperback $15.00
($20.00 Can.)
ISBN: 978-0-9792500-1-3

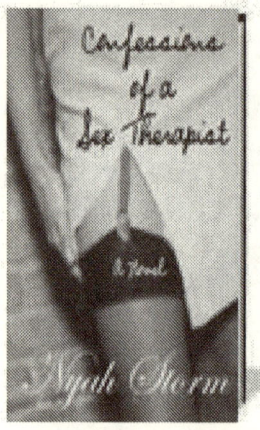

Paperback $15.00
($20.00 Can.)
ISBN: 978-0-9792500-2-6

Paperback $15.00
($20.00 Can.)
ISBN: 978-0-9792500-3-3

Paperback $15.00
($20.00 Can.)
ISBN: 978-0-9722990-4-6